The Subject

Brooke Strahan

The Subject/ Brooke Strahan. -- 1st ed.
ISBN 978-0-6481379-3-1

Contents

I would like to thank Single Hit Armaments and Lieutenant Colonel Alberto Campagnolo for the technical advice, and a big shout out to those 'special' people who helped along the way (you know who you are).

Above all else, guard your heart

—PROV. 4:23

CHAPTER 1

South Melbourne, Victoria

"Y OU NEED TO LOSE two percent body fat," The Agency's director Cheryl informed Bianca. "I want you smoking hot, Bianca. It's been a few weeks since your last subject and its showing."

Bianca looked at herself in the floor-length mirror to her right. She didn't think she needed to lose any weight. Her fit and lean frame was a mere fifty-seven kilograms, and at 5'10" tall she was considered underweight according to any normal BMI.

Cheryl continued on: "This subject has a wife and children. The wife is good looking and smart so you need to be on top of your game."

"Don't worry," Bianca replied. "I will be."

"You can't be so complacent, Bianca," stated Cheryl sternly, looking at her. "This subject is *different*."

What did she mean this one was different? Bianca wondered. Her subjects were always the same. Same demographic, same background, same personalities. For the most part they may as well be clones. To her, her job wasn't rocket science but a refined, almost clinical process that yielded successful results each time. She knew her shit.

It was Bianca's third year with The Agency and she had successfully completed all the jobs she had been tasked. She was satisfied that all the subjects were generally like the one before. But that didn't prevent a job from being interesting, and often fulfilling. She couldn't deny the extra perks that more commonly than not satisfied her.

Bianca's mind wandered as her measurements were being taken and her teeth checked.

"Open wide," Cheryl said, as if she was a dentist. Cheryl stuck some gloved fingers in her mouth and started prodding around. Bianca wondered how Cheryl would react if she suddenly closed her mouth, biting her boss's fingers off. She laughed at the vision and a smile crept across her face.

"What's so funny?"

"Oh, nothing." Bianca thought she had better wipe the grin off her face.

She recalled the first day she had met Cheryl. Bianca was seeing out her last days on the RAAF base while her discharge was being processed. She had loved her job as a Signals Operator Linguist. Her multilingualism and qualitative mindset made the Corporal good at her job. She also exceeded in physical training, and it showed as her arse hadn't ended up looking as if she was smuggling a couple of wombats down there, unlike most of the other service women.

Her love for her job and the Australian Defence Force (ADF) in general did, however, end in one night. The night she was allegedly raped by eight of her supposed 'comrades'. That night changed everything; well, everything but the size of her backside. Comrade. Bianca hated that word now. She preferred other words like *asshole*, *prick* and *cunt*. She thought it ironic that the word beginning with 'c' that she used to call them had been replaced with the other that she used to loathe.

The ADF had sold her a load of broken promises. *Esprit de corps* - what a load of bullshit! The ADF did nothing for her, nothing but give her hush money and a discharge. She was basically told to shut her mouth and her legs. Thinking about it made Bianca's blood boil, and she could feel her skin turning red.

"You okay?" Cheryl asked, now investigating Bianca's face for any sign of a blemish.

"As always, I'm just fine," Bianca replied, trying to calm down her thoughts.

"That's good to hear, but we need you to be more than *just fine*," stated Cheryl as she continued on with the wellness check.

Bianca remembered feeling a sense of utter loss when she was told the RAAF were going to discharge her. Her life had been shattered into a million pieces and she thought it would be such a struggle to put it back together again. She questioned her own decision making and she wondered if it really was of all her own doing?

When Cheryl had first walked up to her, Bianca didn't recognise the high ranking officer. She paid her superior the usual

formalities, but this unexpected visit made her curious as to
its intent.

The officer spoke to Bianca: "You know, Corporal, there are
opportunities for a woman like you outside the government. I
would like to discuss some of these with you, but not here of
course."

Bianca agreed and arrangements were made to meet with
the female officer the following day at a small café in the
city. She hadn't met the officer while on base and wondered
how she had known Bianca was being discharged. She'd
guessed that word had got around, despite the fact the incident was supposed to be completely classified. One thing for
sure that Bianca had learnt, was that the RAAF was one big
cesspool.

"As I said yesterday, there are opportunities for a person like
yourself, if you are open to them," Cheryl had said, smiling at
Bianca.

Bianca looked down at her flat white coffee and stirred it,
despite not taking sugar. "At this point, I think I'm open to
pretty much anything Ma'am," Bianca replied, sighing.

"Good," said Cheryl. "That's what I wanted to hear. You can
relax the formalities, I'm not even a member of the RAAF."

Cheryl could read the look of surprise and confusion on
Bianca's face. "It is part of what I do, Bianca, part of what *we*
do. Pretty good at it, aren't I?"

Cheryl smiled and glanced around the coffee shop. There
was a barista trying not to burn his milk and a young girl
manning the counter. Cheryl noted the girl was preoccupied

with taking an order from an older woman who appeared to not know the difference between a latte and a cappuccino.

Knowing that their meeting would not draw unwanted attention, Cheryl leaned in. "Bianca, I run a very small boutique agency that specialises in information acquirement. Oh and by the way, my name is Cheryl." She took a sip of her coffee and leaned back into her chair looking the epitome of what a woman should represent.

Bianca studied Cheryl properly for the first time since their meeting the day before. She really was quite beautiful. Fit and supple for her age, she must have been at least ten years Bianca's senior.

After a little longer than a moment, Bianca finally spoke, computing both Cheryl's beauty and what was just said to her. "Yes, actually you are. You had me fooled."

Cheryl laughed and smiled warmly, "Don't feel bad about it. If you come and work for me, you'll soon be worthy of academy award nominations too."

Bianca just sat there. She was used to interpreting signals that made no sense to most people. This conversation was, however, in plain English; yet Bianca was struggling to grasp it. Cheryl continued, "The Agency is the only one of its kind in Australia and we only employ the most suitable candidates. We are very small, but specialised. It's all about quality not quantity with us." Cheryl leaned back with an air of confidence and certainty. "I believe that you would make a suitable candidate... if this position interests you?"

Bianca noticed how Cheryl had raised an eyebrow when

asking the question. Her eyebrows were perfectly shaped. Bianca suddenly felt conscious of her own less well-groomed brows.

"What information, exactly, would I be acquiring?" Bianca asked, getting over her eyebrow insecurity.

"Ah ha," Cheryl said lowering her voice. "Now this is where it gets interesting. However, I am not going to spell it out in a place like this. I know for a fact you are a smart woman, Bianca; you should be able to work it out." Cheryl took another sip of her cappuccino, looking more relaxed than ever.

Bianca sat there shocked, her flat white lowering in temperature by the minute. *Was she hearing this for real?*

"So I would be a spy?" she finally asked Cheryl, still trying to comprehend the seriousness of what she had just heard.

Cheryl glanced around the café again, suddenly looking a lot more serious. "We prefer not to use that word, Bianca; that's a swear word in my company. You won't have a job if you use it again, understood?"

"Understood," Bianca stated, nodding her head. She had been in the RAAF for long enough to know an order when she heard one.

"You have terrible situational awareness," Cheryl snapped. "However, we can work on that."

Bianca looked around her. The coffee shop was now starting to fill up with the Saturday morning crowd ordering their soy lattes and reading the newspaper. No one had even turned their head her way. But then, maybe they had and she simply hadn't noticed.

"Listen, Bianca," Cheryl said in a very low and almost scary tone. "What has this government done for you? Nothing. It has done nothing but screw you over, quite literally. Am I right?"

Cheryl was right. Bianca had served for five years and given nothing but her heart and soul to the RAAF and all they had done was eat her up and spit her out, as if she was nothing. Nothing but a piece of fucking meat. Bianca thought how the ADF resembled one large butcher's shop.

"Bianca, at The Agency, we will give you a purpose. You will have a whole new career. You will be given some of the best training to ensure you can perform your role competently, but also safely. Our operators are the forefront of our business. We do everything we can to ensure their success and safety. This is a very special role for a very special person," Cheryl stated, playing to Bianca's narcissism. Cheryl took another sip of her cappuccino and continued, "There's a position for you if you want it. If not, you can walk away now and this conversation never happened."

Bianca looked down into her almost cold flat white as if it was a crystal ball that would reveal to her what she should do. She then remembered how she felt when she had been called 'a groundsheet'.

Mother fuckers, she thought.

"I'll do it," Bianca said with absolute conviction.

"That a girl," replied Cheryl with a smile. "Hell hath no fury like a woman scorned. I have full faith in your abilities."

"Did you hear me, Bianca?" asked Cheryl. "You may find this subject a challenge."

"I heard you. I will lose the body fat."

"Good. And clean those dirty fingernails, you're such a bug."

Bitch, Bianca thought. Cheryl had, however, spoken some truth. Her fingernails were pretty disgusting. Bianca let them be dirty for a reason, though. The dirty fingernails kept her more real. It made her appear like a normal down-to-earth woman who wasn't afraid to do some house and yard work. That was appealing to the majority of men, plus it actually was the truth apart from the fact her apartment didn't have a yard.

Cheryl walked out of the room, dropping Bianca's job file on the desk. Bianca was glad her routine wellness check at The Agency was over. She didn't mind the reporting process of the information she had acquired, nor did she mind the ongoing training or her job briefings. They were all vital parts of the job with which she was tasked. She just hated the wellness checks. Apparently they were designed to make sure she was physically and aesthetically up to standard for the role. It made her feel like a Russian model wannabe being scrutinised at an international modelling agency. Bianca never showed any sign of weakness or discomfort during them. She knew it was part of the job and as such had to be endured. Whenever they wanted her to come in, The Agency would summon her and Bianca would come as requested. She was never to come to The Agency of her own accord, never. That had been made very clear from the beginning.

Bianca picked up her job file and opened it up. It read 'Subject Name: Thomas Christian'.

So, Mr Christian, she thought, *I guess I'll be seeing you very soon.*

CHAPTER 2

Inner Eastern Suburbs, Melbourne, Victoria

B IANCA WALKED INTO THE trendy coffee shop. In true
Melbourne style, the weather was far from impressive,
so she was wearing her favourite black leather jacket. She had
teamed it with her skinny leg jeans, black calf-length boots and
a large designer handbag.

It was her first time entering the coffee shop, although
everything about it was familiar. The noise, the smells, the
people. Bianca had been studying the shop for over a week now.
The reason for the study? Because her newest subject, Thomas
Christian, could frequently be found there.

Thomas had retired a couple of years ago from the Victorian
Police, or VICPOL as it is known. He had spent the past fifteen
years of his service in the Special Operations Group (SOG) and
he had retired as a Senior Sergeant. Bianca guessed that the
admin associated with the Senior Sergeant's role had bored
him, especially after all those years in the field.

Thomas appeared to be writing a book, or some epic thesis. Bianca had not quite got a close enough look to determine which it was. Either way, it didn't matter. All that mattered was that she knew this was his favourite little spot to tap away on his laptop while ordering multiple coffees and flirting with the young waitresses.

"Oh my God, I am *so* sorry!" Bianca exclaimed, looking embarrassed. "I am such a friggin' klutz."

Bianca wasn't a klutz. She had purposely placed her large tote bag on her shoulder and then suddenly turned around next to Thomas's table. Her bag hit his coffee cup and sent it flying. Coffee spilled across the table, narrowly missing his laptop.

"It's okay, don't worry about it," Thomas said, but Bianca could tell he was annoyed at the spillage.

Thomas hadn't looked up. He was too busy trying to mop up the mess with his napkin.

"Let me buy you a new one," Bianca remarked, to make amends. "What do you have, a flat white?"

This time Thomas looked up. He stared at Bianca. He could see that Bianca was younger than him, but not by much. She was dressed for the weather, but he couldn't help notice that there was a body under all those clothes. Her brunette hair didn't appear to be styled, but still perfectly cascaded over her shoulders. Her brown eyes were staring back at him.

"I'll take you up on that. And yes, I'll have a flat white."

"Sure thing," Bianca replied as she walked over to the service counter. Bianca could feel Thomas's eyes on her backside.

Cheryl had told her that her butt was one of her best assets and it should be utilised as much as humanly possible.

Thomas admired the woman from a distance as she ordered his fresh coffee. He felt a flush of guilt go through him. He was a married man, and not just that, he had a couple of kids too. He really needed to try to stop looking at other women like this.

"Here you go," Bianca said, placing the hot flat white in front of Thomas. She shifted her body weight as if she was about to leave.

"Hey if you want to, you can join me if you like? I need a break from this," said Thomas, looking at his laptop and the open Word document. His guilt had obviously just been momentary.

"Well, I was just going to get a takeaway coffee, but I guess I have some time."

Bianca pulled up the chair across from Thomas. He saved his document and shut the lid of the laptop so he could concentrate on the woman with the apparent passion fingers. A cute waitress came straight over and took Bianca's order. *Geez,* Bianca thought, *the service is good here.*

"I'm Thomas, but my friends all call me Christo."

"Why do they call you Christo?" Bianca asked, looking into her subject's light blue eyes.

"Because my surname is Christian."

"Well that makes sense," Bianca said with a little laugh. Ever since she was a little girl, she often finished a sentence with a little laugh. She had been told it had something to do with nervous tension.

Thomas studied her face. It was not perfect, but it was perfect for *her*.

Bianca knew she didn't have a perfect face. Cheryl had often told her that. "But your body makes up for it," was a regular line from her boss's mouth. The Agency had offered to pay for her to have rhinoplasty, which Bianca declined. Cheryl seemed to accept that fairly easily, which surprised Bianca considering how high Cheryl's expectations were of her. She did, however, make Bianca have BOTOX injected regularly into her face. She couldn't get out of that one using her fear of going under anaesthetic as an excuse. Initially Bianca had protested, "You know, Cheryl, botulinum toxin is a biological warfare agent; apparently Iraq was producing it in litres during the Gulf War!" Unfortunately, Cheryl didn't seem to care about Bianca's opinion on the poison and she was made to have needles containing it stuck into her facial muscles.

"My name is Bianca, Bianca Beretta."

"Beretta, huh?" Thomas said with an interested look on his face. "They make good guns, you know?"

"I wouldn't know anything about that," Bianca lied. "It's an Italian surname - the first Mayor of Milan was a Beretta."

"That's interesting. I like interesting facts," Thomas said with a smile that moved Bianca more than she preferred.

"You working today?" Bianca asked waving her hand towards his laptop.

"No, not really. Some might call it work, but I don't."

"What do you call it then?" asked Bianca, suddenly intrigued.

"I call it *therapy*."

"Do you mind me asking why you need therapy, I mean if that's not *too* personal?" Bianca asked, leaning in a touch closer and picking up the coffee that had just appeared in front of her.

"Well, after eighteen years with the Victorian Police, you would probably need therapy too!"

Bianca laughed. "Yes, well, I guess a job like that would be pretty stressful, but I'm sure it was rewarding too?"

"I wasn't really rewarded for the most part. Not long after I joined, I became a SOGGIE, so no-one even really knew what I did," Thomas said, adding a spoonful of sugar to his coffee.

"Sugar is the devil," Bianca remarked. "What's a SOGGIE?"

"It's the name given to a member of the Special Operations Group, and yes I know sugar is the devil, but we all have our vices, right?"

Bianca raised her eyebrows at him. Her eyebrows were now groomed, Cheryl had made sure of that. Ignoring the vices comment, Bianca replied in a derisive tone, "Special Operations Group, ooh sounds *special.*"

"Don't be like that," Thomas rebutted, a little taken aback by the hot stranger's mocking tone.

Bianca smiled inside. She could tell that despite only meeting minutes ago, her opinion mattered to him. This was a good sign, and a good start to her job.

"Oh, I'm sorry, I didn't mean to sound disrespectful, I'm sure you performed a *very* important job."

"Don't worry about it. I can take being made fun of. I'm just not used to it from someone I just met." Thomas took a swig of his flat white and continued, "This coffee is better than the last, glad you spilt it."

Bianca smiled and turned slightly away as she knew she was blushing. Regaining her composure, she asked, "So what's the therapy you are undertaking?"

"I'm writing a book. It's a very cathartic process. It's a fiction novel, but I'm using my time with the police for the inspiration."

"Sounds like a bestseller to me," Bianca stated in a matter-of-fact tone.

"We'll see."

Bianca smiled again at her subject and stood up as she took the last mouthful of her coffee. She realised how quickly she had downed the beverage.

"You going already?" asked Thomas looking disappointed.

"Yes, I have to be somewhere soon - and I'm not sure if I should be having coffee with a married man," Bianca was looking directly at the band of white gold on Thomas's left hand.

Thomas felt slightly ashamed, but he quickly put that feeling aside. "Correct, I am married, but I don't see a problem with having a coffee with someone. Good company and good conversation is good company and good conversation, be it man or woman, young or old."

Bianca couldn't really argue with that, nor did she want to.

"Well, Mr Christian, you got me there." A big white smile flashed across her face.

Thomas noticed how perfect her skin was. It appeared to be evenly tanned and each random freckle spoke to him, telling its own story.

"I hang out here a lot," Thomas informed Bianca. "The coffee isn't always the best, but they have good service and I just like the vibe, it's good for my writing."

"A bit of a muse then, hey?" Bianca asked almost suggestively.

"I haven't found my muse... *yet*," Thomas replied, his eyes piercing Bianca like a bullet from her namesake. "But I am looking..."

"Aren't we all," Bianca riposted with a sly smile as she left Thomas sitting at the table.

Now Thomas was blushing. He didn't blush easily and he was surprised at how this woman had stirred something inside him from the get-go.

Bianca walked out the coffee shop door. She felt Thomas's eyes follow her onto the street until she disappeared into the crowd and traffic. *Cheryl had been right*, Bianca thought. *There was something different about this subject.* Despite him being in the same demographic as the majority of her past studies, there was something about him she just couldn't put her finger on. Bianca decided she wasn't going to be worried with that right now; she was just looking forward to hopefully being able to get more than a finger on him.

CHAPTER 3

Inner Eastern Suburbs, Melbourne, Victoria

"**Y**OU COME HERE OFTEN?"
Bianca immediately recognised the voice.

"Oh God, you've got to have a better line than that, don't you?" Bianca retorted, happy to hear Thomas's voice.

"Ah, no not really, this is about as good as it gets." He was telling the truth. He had never been great with pick-up lines, but despite this seemed to have had no problem getting women.

"Well no, I don't come here often, but that might be changing. You see, I don't mind the coffee or the décor..."

"Good to see you again, Bianca," said Thomas, more than pleased she was in the coffee shop again.

"Likewise."

Bianca looked Thomas up and down. He was not a giant of a man, but he still had presence. He actually commanded some type of attention, despite appearing sedate. His hair was slightly longer than he would have worn it in the police force; and he was unshaven, obviously trying to show off his new-found liberties as a civilian. His laptop bag was slung across his body and he wore a plain white t-shirt with jeans that fitted as though they had been made just for him. The Melbourne weather was behaving in its usual way, so a grey wool duffle jacket with epaulettes finished off his outfit.

Not bad, Bianca thought. She noticed two mothers with their prams looking over at them, particularly Thomas. She glared back at them and they quickly turned their glance away and returned to talking about shitty nappies or whatever it is that new mothers talk about.

"So," Thomas said. "Um, can I join you?"

"Oh, I'm sorry, I thought you had come in here to undertake some more *therapy*," Bianca said, staring at Thomas's laptop bag.

"Well that was the plan, but like any good plan, one should be able to adapt it to the changing situation."

"Sounds like police talk to me, but yes, you can join me if you like," and with that Bianca pushed out the chair across from her with her leather booted leg.

Fuck, she has long legs, Thomas thought, remembering how he had always wanted longer legs himself. It would have made getting over all those obstacles so much easier. Thomas sat down, took off his jacket and placed it on the back of his chair.

"So how is the book project going?" Bianca asked as she took a sip of her flat white. It was almost all gone. Thomas had arrived later than she had anticipated, despite her time studying his movements around the coffee shop.

"Yeah, it's going," Thomas answered with a sigh.

"By the sound of that answer, you mean, 'don't ask'."

"Yep, pretty much."

"Sounds like you need a coffee. A flat white again?" Bianca went to get up, but Thomas stopped her.

"No, I'll get it. You want another one?"

Bianca looked at her now empty cup, thinking she must learn not to drink so fast.

"Yeah, sure, why not?"

Thomas noticed the smile Bianca gave him. It was a really cute smile.

"Let me guess what you will have, a mochaccino?"

"Yuck, no, you don't ruin coffee with putting chocolate in it!" Bianca blurted out. "I'm the same as you, remember - flat white, but *I* don't have sugar."

Thomas knew what she was getting at. He recalled her 'Sugar is the devil' comment from the other day. *It was true, though*, he concurred. *That stuff should be illegal*. It was more addictive and definitely more dangerous than many of the other illicit drugs. He had put on a couple of kilos since retirement despite his regular gym workouts and various other types of training. He thought maybe he should try not to have sugar in his coffee.

Thomas ordered the two coffees at the counter. He knew he could have waited at the table to be served, but he wanted to check his phone discreetly, as he had felt a vibration through his pocket a moment ago. Thomas looked over at Bianca. She seemed to be looking out the window, people watching.

Thomas read the text: *Your appointment is scheduled at 1500hrs tomorrow.* He closed the message, locked his phone and put it back into his pocket.

"So I ordered you a big slice of that chocolate mud cake to go along with your coffee," Thomas joked as he pointed to the cake display stand that housed a number of delicious looking desserts. Thomas could have ordered a slice of one of each for himself, but he thought he'd better not in front of Bianca, as she seemed like a bit of a sugar Nazi. He wondered if she was one of those 'clean eating' freaks, and hoped she wasn't. He couldn't stand people with self-appointed dietary requirements.

Bianca glared at him. She knew he hadn't ordered her the cake. She had seen his movements in the window reflection and there were no indications that cake was coming her way. He had appeared to quickly order the coffee and look at his phone. The cake comment was just the man trying to be funny. She thought he'd better stick to writing a book rather than being a comedian, if his book was not supposed to be humorous - and if it was, it would probably be a flop.

The coffee shop had changed its CD and now Adele was playing over the speakers and the din of the café. The song *Someone like You* had come on. Bianca cringed.

"I can't stand Adele," she commented.

Thomas looked surprised. He thought everyone liked Adele, especially chicks. "Why is that?"

"Shotgun music. You know, the type of music that is so depressing that when you listen to it you just want to put a shotgun in your mouth and blow your brains out!"

"Wow, okay then. I guess come to think about it, she is pretty depressing."

A young waitress walked over in a skirt too short for hospitality. "Here's your flat whites."

"Can I ask a favour - can you change the CD to something else please?"

Bianca focused her eyes on Thomas. It was one of the nicest things anyone had ever done for her.

The waitress looked at him strangely, but answered, "Yeah, sure, I guess."

Thomas was looking at Bianca and she could tell he was pleased with himself for making such a confident move.

"You didn't have to do that," Bianca remarked, taking a sip of her hot flat white. It was actually too hot and she felt her tongue burn.

"Yeah I did, we couldn't have you offing yourself now, could we?"

Bianca just smiled and Thomas smiled back. She felt the tension between them growing, but it wasn't a bad tension, it was a good tension. She liked it more than she knew she should.

"I know you said not to ask about your book, but I was just thinking that if you are having writer's block or something like that, maybe you could tell me some of your police stories and that might bring back some memories and give you some inspiration?"

Thomas looked thoughtful. "That's not a bad idea actually. But I'm not sure if I feel like telling any of my war stories today.

I'm more interested in hearing about *you*." He took a sip of his flat white. It must have been too hot as well because it looked as if he was in pain, but trying not to show it.

"A bit hot, yeah?" Bianca laughed.

"You're not wrong, you could have told me!" Thomas exclaimed.

"Ah, sorry, I thought you were tough, you know - being all Special Forces and all that."

Thomas quickly corrected her. "Not Special Forces, Special Operations Group. One is military and the other is police. Completely different."

"Oh, I see, my bad. But you are still *special*, right?" Bianca laughed at her own condescendence.

Thomas wasn't overly impressed at her comment. He had worked hard to be a member of SOG and now the stranger was making fun of him, *again*. Thomas quickly put his hurt feelings aside. He concluded that obviously Bianca had no idea about the job or what it involved. She was probably a hairdresser or something.

Pete Murray was now playing over the café speakers.

Much better, thought Bianca. *We won't be having another café incident today.* There had been too many of them in Australia in recent years.

Thomas picked up the sachet of sugar from the little jar on the table. He was about to open it when he remembered Bianca's opinion of the white granulated demon. He quickly put the sugar down.

"No sugar today, huh?"

"No, I'm sweet enough today." Thomas immediately regretted saying that.

Bianca coughed. "Dad joke." *Cough, cough.*

"Well, I am a Dad!" He immediately regretted that one too. *What was it with this woman?* He thought. She seemed to make him say things he usually wouldn't. He would never usually tell a hot chick that he had kids - well not straight up.

Bianca seemed nonchalant. "Not surprising, everyone does." Thomas glared at her. "That is, everyone but me." Bianca decided to try her flat white again. This time the temperature was somewhat drinkable.

Thomas realised that apart from her name, this was the first bit of information he had about Bianca. Actually, he did know something else: she was a flat white drinking, sugar hating leather wearer. *No kids*, he thought. *She is obviously half switched on.* Not like the majority of bimbos he had met during his life. All they seemed to want to do was have babies. Even his wife, who Thomas was proud to say was not a bimbo, had wanted children. Thomas hadn't really wanted kids, but he went along with it anyway. He had always been told 'happy wife, happy life'. He had, however, quickly learnt that both don't necessarily go hand-in-hand.

"Bianca, do you drink wine?"

"Yes."

"Red? White? Sparkling?"

"Yes."

"I mean, I'm asking which one you prefer."

"Thomas, when it comes to wine, 'yes' is my answer."

Thomas pondered on this for a moment before speaking. "Oh I see, so you are a bit of wine connoisseur, then?" He was interested in her answer, as he was quite partial to a wine himself.

"Well I am half Italian, but no, not a connoisseur, probably more like an alcoholic."

They both laughed and the tension between them heightened. Bianca's skin felt clammy, but Thomas thought it was glowing. He wanted to touch it, to see what it felt like, but he knew better than to be so forward.

Bianca took another sip of her coffee. She had waited long enough for it to come to a drinkable temperature so she thought it best not to let it go cold. "Why do you ask?"

"Because I thought I might see if you want to have a drink with me, I mean something a bit nicer than this coffee." He looked down at his coffee and he could feel the nervousness through his body. Nervous for Bianca's answer, but also nervous at the fact he was doing something a married man really shouldn't do. It was a good nervous, though. He loved his wife and his children, but he had cheated before, quite a number of times. He had felt guilty and excited at the same time. He remembered thinking he would surely go to hell and that same thought again passed through his mind. He quickly shrugged it off, remembering his old work motto: 'Blessed are the peacemakers'. He was blessed, he thought. Heck, he had been a SOGGIE - *Son of God*. He definitely didn't need to worry about his sins.

"Well, you do have writer's block, so I guess I can help you out with getting your artistic juices flowing. You might be able to tell me some of your stories and I'll tell you some of mine," Bianca remarked, lying once again.

"Oh, what stories do *you* have to tell?" Thomas asked in a flirting manner. His light blue eyes were gazing at Bianca and for a moment she almost lost herself in them.

She regained her steely composure. "You'll just have to wait to find out."

CHAPTER 4

Outer Eastern Suburbs, Melbourne, Victoria

AFTER PICKING UP SOME groceries, Bianca was relieved to be back at her apartment. She fucking hated the grocery store. She hated the screaming toddlers who had been told they weren't having that lolly. She hated the glances of other shoppers who judged her shopping cart in an instant and she hated most of all the trolleys that never travelled in a straight line. On many occasions Bianca had thought that an aircraft must be easier to navigate than a shopping trolley, flashing back to her flight theory lessons when she was a member of the Australian Air League, before she had joined the RAAF.

She poured herself a Sauvignon Blanc. She felt blessed to be living in Godzone. Not because of the open plains or amazing coastline, or even the opportunities. It was just because Australia had the best wines. White, red, whatever, they were all usually good. She had travelled overseas and their wines were less than pleasing to her palette or, as she often described them, 'crap'.

Bianca kicked off her boots and plonked herself on the lounge with her wineglass that resembled a fishbowl. She turned on the TV. There was a lady with a smile too big for her own face trying to sell her some fridge storage containers. The big-smile lady disappeared as Bianca changed the channel. She settled on a cooking show. Bianca wasn't the best cook herself, especially for an Italian, but she thought if she watched enough Food Network maybe she'd miraculously become the next Giada De Laurentiis.

Samson, her Siamese cat, jumped up on the couch and looked at her with his stunning blue eyes.

Eyes like Thomas, Bianca thought as she stroked the silky furred feline. After about a minute of stroking, Samson had obviously had enough and jumped off the couch and onto the armchair in the corner, where he proceeded to follow his tail in circles in the same spot on the chair until he settled into just the right position. Samson started purring.

That cat does not give a fuck about anything. Bianca thought how much she could learn from the animal.

Beep - her Samsung Galaxy phone lit up. She picked it up and saw it was a text from Thomas. Bianca felt a flush of excitement come over her.

Thursday 8pm @ De Levitas, is what the text read.

Good taste, Bianca thought as she took a big sip of her wine. She could feel it entering her blood and began to feel more relaxed after the trauma of the grocery store.

Bianca text back: *See you then.*

Immediately she received another text from Thomas: *Looking forward to it, night X.*

'X' - what the fuck! Bianca couldn't believe he had sent her a kiss symbol already. He was game; that was for sure. She hoped he had immediately deleted his texts, just in case his wife checked his phone and screwed everything up.

The cooking show was boring and she found her mind wandering. Her thoughts were of Thomas. This was new for her. Once home, she usually switched off from work and any thoughts of her subjects. Bianca knew better than to develop any real emotional attachment to them. That was because she never really knew what happened to them after her job was done. She had not asked Cheryl or any of the other staff at The Agency. Bianca thought it best to remain ignorant, and it wasn't her place to ask anyway. *Maybe nothing happened to them? Maybe once the client was happy with the information acquired then the subject just carried on with their life, none the wiser.* Despite trying to be optimistic, there was always a feeling that this possibly wasn't always the case. *Who knew what a client did with the information they obtained or what this meant for the subject?* She shuddered. This was why she couldn't get emotionally involved; it would mess her up.

Bianca went to her panties drawer and pulled out a grey case. She needed to get her mind off Thomas. She entered a code and the case unlocked. Inside was a Beretta 92 pistol. It was a sweet looking piece of weaponry. She also liked it because it was the same as her name, as if it had been made just for her.

At the Agency she had been given her choice of side arm. She was offered a Browning GP-35, Glock 22 and even the Heckler & Koch USP, but the Beretta 92 was naturally her weapon of choice.

The Agency had trained her on the pistol, plus the other standard firearms as well, just in case. She had been told it was completely up to her if she carried the concealed weapon with her on her jobs or not. If she did her job properly there really should be no need to carry a firearm, as the majority of jobs had a low risk assessment attached. This was certainly the case for the most part, but Bianca still remembered the words she was told in regard to the carrying of the firearm: *user discretion.*

Bianca took another swig of her wine. She knew she probably shouldn't clean it under the influence, but going through the motions of field stripping the pistol, cleaning the working parts and putting it back together again gave her something to concentrate on.

The magazine was sitting separately in the case from the pistol. Bianca picked up the pistol and immediately checked the chamber to make sure it was empty. She thought that would be the most embarrassing thing ever, to have to admit that you had accidentally shot yourself! If that ever happened, Bianca had already decided that she would have to shoot herself again, but this time in the head because she wouldn't be able to live with the embarrassment. She pulled the slide all the way back and locked it with the slide stop lever, depressed the takedown lever stop and rotated the takedown lever at the same time. She pulled the slide slightly back and then pushed it forward, allowing it to come out of the frame. Bianca removed the return spring and pushed the locking lever pin, allowing her to lift the barrel up from the slide.

Bianca looked at the bits and pieces scattered around her on the bedroom floorboards. They looked so innocent just lying there, almost like pieces of modern Lego that a child had not bothered to put away after his playtime. But they weren't innocent and they most certainly were not toys. They were pieces of technology that, once put together correctly, had one purpose. To kill. Bianca hated it when she heard people say things like: "I don't understand why the police didn't just shoot him in the leg. Why did they have to kill him?" She had to show the utmost restraint and bite her tongue when all she really wanted to say was: "If you had any idea on anything, you would know that when you are trained on a firearm you are trained to take out the motherfucker."

Bianca took her time cleaning the parts, in between polishing off the bottle of the wine. She put the pistol back together and looked at her floorboards that were once again Lego-free.

All shiny and new, Bianca thought, admiring her handiwork. She checked the time on her Android. *Shit*, it was later than she had thought and she had forgotten to eat - again.

Oh well, I guess the wine was my dinner, Bianca thought, laughing at her own joke.

She picked up the freshly serviced Beretta. "Tap and rack," she said to herself as she inserted the magazine she had loaded followed by a pull of the slide back, allowing for the bullet to enter the chamber. She ensured the safety was on and placed the sidearm on a small concealed shelf under her bed, where it slept with her every night. Bianca had made a promise to herself that never would she not be able to defend herself against anything or anyone.

South Melbourne, Victoria

"Thomas, you're late. You were meant to be here at 1500 hours."

"Sorry, Cheryl, I was writing my book and I got caught up in it and lost track of time."

"Oh yes, your book - that's right. You know better than to put anything it in that even resembles your job here at The Agency, don't you?"

"Of course. I'm not an idiot," Thomas snapped back.

"No need to use that tone with me. I was just giving you a friendly reminder." She smiled at him and continued, "I thought you had writer's block anyway. You've found some new inspiration, have you?" Cheryl looked at him with her raised and perfectly shaped eyebrow.

"Yeah, I met this girl..." Thomas's voice faded off.

"Oh God, not another girl. You just can't keep it in your pants, can you?" Cheryl sounded almost jealous. "Imagine what your wife would think."

"What she doesn't know doesn't hurt her."

Cheryl huffed. David, The Agency's Operations Manager, walked over to Thomas.

"Did I just hear you right - you got another chick on the side?"

David asked, sounding a bit too interested.

David was short and partially bald. Thomas wasn't sure what David had done before working for The Agency and he didn't particularly care. He didn't, however, look like ex-police or ex-military, not even Navy.

Whenever Thomas was at The Agency, David seemed to follow him around like a puppy dog, despite being his superior. Thomas thought it was odd behaviour and it annoyed him a bit, but there wasn't much he could do about it. He always seemed overly interested in Thomas's sex life. It had even crossed Thomas's mind that David might still be a virgin.

"So what's she like? Bet she's hot. You always get the hot ones," David asked, waiting in anticipation for the answer.

"Mate, I'd drink her bath water."

David laughed. "You're a sicko, Christo. Good one."

The men laughed together. "Boys!" snapped Cheryl. "Stop that smut and get in the boardroom. Thomas, you need to give us a full briefing from your studies. After that you have your wellness check." With her Surface Pro in her hands, Cheryl walked out of the room and towards the boardroom.

"Coming," yelled Thomas.

"Bet you will be saying that sooner rather than later with your new chick, ha ha." David seemed pleased with his own joke. Thomas just shook his head and thought, *Yep, he is definitely a virgin.*

CHAPTER 5

Inner City, Melbourne, Victoria

THOMAS WAS ONTO HIS second glass of wine and she hadn't arrived yet. He would normally have started with a beer and then moved onto a red wine with dinner, but since she seemed to possibly be a wine snob he straight up ordered an expensive bottle of De Bortoli for the table.

She'd better like it, he thought.

He glanced at the Tissot sitting on his wrist. She was twenty-five minutes late. He was starting to feel like an idiot. *What was he doing?* It felt as if a blanket of guilt was starting to suffocate him as he thought of the lie he had told his wife about having to do nightshift again as head of security for a large commercial building in the city. The blanket suddenly disappeared when he saw Bianca walk into the restaurant.

Stunner, he thought as the waiter showed her to the table where Thomas was seated.

"Glad to see you, Bianca. You look beautiful."

Bianca did look beautiful. She wore a dress she had bought

on Chapel Street paired with her expensive Louboutin heels. The dress wasn't revealing, yet it made Thomas's imagination run wild. He pictured ripping it off her there and then and throwing her on the table.

Thomas gave her a kiss on the cheek. The tension was so thick you would have needed a knife to cut it. He felt some hardness in his nether regions and immediately sat down, embarrassed by his lack of control.

"Thank you." Bianca replied, "You look nice too."

Nice? thought Thomas, *Is that all I get?* He had made a real effort getting ready, and he'd had to do it in his car! He couldn't have left the house dressed up like that, no way, not unless he wanted a divorce, and he couldn't afford that.

"Thank you. I ordered us a bottle of wine already…"

"I see that," Bianca interrupted him, staring at the almost half-empty bottle on the table.

"Would you like a glass?" Thomas started pouring the liquid gold into her wineglass before Bianca had a chance to answer. She didn't mind because of course her answer would have been "yes."

"Thank you. So what have you been up to?"

"Oh you know, the usual. Working on the book, going to the gym, trying not to have sugar in my coffee, ha ha," Thomas laughed, and Bianca just stared at him. He felt like a bit of a dork.

She finally spoke, "Working on your book, hey? That's good to hear. So your writer's block is gone?" She was hoping the answer was no.

"No, it's not gone, but it's positively improved the past few days. I've been *inspired*."

Bianca felt relieved. Him telling her his "war stories" was an easy way to get information out of him without having to resort to some of her other blagging tactics.

The waiter came over to the table. He looked eager to please and Bianca wondered how long he'd worked there.

"Good evening, are you ready to place your order?"

"We haven't even looked at the menu yet, sorry," Thomas answered.

"So you would like me to give you a few minutes more?" The young waiter asked.

"Please."

Bianca was impressed at Thomas's social graces. He obviously was a chameleon. Much like herself, she thought. She suddenly imagined him throwing a flashbang into a room where the offenders were, and she could hear him screaming at them to get their "fucking hands on their fucking heads, now!" That is, of course, if they hadn't already been shot.

"The lamb sounds good," commented Thomas. He suddenly had a thought. *Crap, what if she's a vegetarian, or even worse one of those people who didn't eat gluten?* He hadn't even bothered to ask, but then he hadn't really bothered to ask anything really. He thought for a moment that maybe he was starting to lose his mojo.

"Yeah it does, but I will go the seafood marinara. I'm a bit of a seafood fan."

"That's good to hear," Thomas said with relief in his voice. "I was worried you might have been one of those people who don't eat pasta."

"What, a coeliac? Unlikely. I've never met an Italian who can't eat gluten."

Thomas deliberated on her answer. "Come to think of it, neither have I, actually." He took a sip of his wine. "What exactly is gluten?"

"I don't know Thomas, but I know I love it," Bianca replied, thinking back to her Nonna's carbonara that she used to devour in bowlfuls as a young girl when she would visit her in Griffith.

Thomas laughed at her answer. Beneath her façade, she did have a sense of humour. "Don't we all," he said, thinking about his growing waistline. The pair shared a smile across the white cloth that separated them.

The waiter returned to the table. "What will you be having tonight?"

"*Guardi, per me spaghetti ai frutti di mare e per lui agnello al forno con patate, grazie.*"

"*Certamente, con piacere.*" The waiter walked off towards the kitchen, without writing the order down.

Bianca noticed Thomas looking at her in awe as she took a sip of her red wine. She could have finished it in one swig but she thought it best to use some manners.

"I'm guessing you ordered me the lamb then?" Thomas asked, looking bemused. "How did you know he was Italian as well?"

"Well we are in an Italian restaurant. And haven't you noticed? Us Italians, we are just like the Chinese, we all look the same." It took Thomas a moment to realise Bianca was joking. Thomas laughed.

"No, seriously, I liked hearing you speak then, your accent was sexy."

"My Mum sounds just like that," Bianca retorted, shooting him down.

Thomas decided to ignore her comment. She seemed to have trouble taking a compliment, or maybe she just enjoyed making him feel like a doofus. He thought that possibly she had some type of insecurity and this was her defence mechanism. He just hoped she wasn't a real psycho bitch. He had been there and done that, probably too many times. They all seemed nice at the start and then they turned into a crazy bitch, worthy of a medication and a straitjacket.

"You're not a psycho are you, Bianca?" Thomas asked. The words had just fallen out of his mouth.

Bianca almost spat her wine all over his Ralph Lauren shirt. "Excuse me?"

"Sorry, that really didn't come out right. It's just that I've met a lot of women who have turned out to be psychopathic."

Bianca took a moment and another sip of wine. She was really trying her best to make it last. There wasn't another bottle on the table, *yet*.

"Thomas, have you ever wondered that possibly your actions may have triggered something inside the woman to cause her psychopathic behaviour? She actually may have been acting rational given the situation."

Thomas took the wineglass from his lips and put it back on

the table. He looked at Bianca and appeared to be ruminating on her words. He finally answered, shaking his head, "No, not a chance."

Thomas excused himself and made his way to the bathroom. Bianca checked her work phone and was happy to see she had no new messages. She double-checked it was set to silent and slipped it back into her Balenciaga clutch purse.

Thomas returned to the table. Bianca smiled at him. Thomas noticed the smile and he felt butterflies inside. He knew it wasn't really butterflies, but the intestine releasing hydrochloric acid into the small intestine plus a reduction in blood flow, all to deal with the stressor. Bianca was the stressor, but she was a good stressor. He was more than happy to deal with that type of stress, especially when it took on that form.

Their waiter appeared at the table again. This time he was holding their meals. Bianca thought that dinner had come out just a little too quickly for her liking. She knew how long those meals should take, since she was going to be the next food network star!

"Here is your seafood marinara, Ma'am, and here is your lamb, Sir. Enjoy. Please let me know if there is anything else I can get you." The waiter backed away. He was hoping for a tip from the couple, who looked as if they could afford it.

"Another bottle of the same wine?" Bianca asked the waiter. Thomas cringed inside, thinking of the indent in his wallet. Lucky he had a bundle of cash on him. He was smart enough not to put such outings on his VISA card. The young waiter scurried off.

"Now, Thomas, I am actually intrigued about why you asked me out here tonight. What would a married man with children want with me?" Bianca asked, acting innocent and manipulating the conversation.

"To be honest, Bianca, I just feel that I can talk to you. My wife is so busy at home with the kids and everything. She has her friends and the things she likes. Sometimes we don't seem to have anything in common." Thomas looked down at his plate and stuffed a potato into his mouth.

"And you think we have something in common, do you?" Bianca raised one of her eyebrows as much as she could, as her recent BOTOX treatment had kicked in.

Thomas looked at her. He didn't know if they had anything in common. He just hoped maybe there was something. It felt like it, that there was something there.

"She's not even really interested in my book," Thomas sighed. "At least you are a bit interested, aren't you?"

This was the moment Bianca was waiting for. This was her in, but she couldn't seem too keen.

"Yeah, I'm interested. I mean only because I'm a creative type myself. I'm an artist." She curled her pasta around her fork. The seafood marinara was delicious and she wondered what Cheryl would say if she saw such a big serving of carbs on her plate.

"Obviously not a struggling artist, by the look of that dress." Thomas admired the dress, trying not to stare at the seams around the bust.

"Oh, this old thing!" Bianca joked and she laughed her

nervous laugh.

Thomas laughed too and Bianca felt good that he had gone along with her joke.

"An artist, hey? Well, we do have something in common then." Thomas poured Bianca a glass from the new bottle of wine that had appeared at the table thanks to the overzealous waiter. He then poured himself another glass.

"*Salute,*" Bianca said as she raised her glass. There was a *clink* as the wineglasses met in the centre of the table.

CHAPTER 6

Outer Eastern Suburbs, Melbourne, Victoria

B IANCA WOKE WITH A headache. *Fuck, that red wine,* she thought. She needed two things, Panadol and coffee, ASAP!

She didn't think she had drunk that much, plus she had managed to drive home and in one piece. Quickly she pulled back her white sheets and checked herself. *Yes, definitely in one piece.* She felt thankful.

Last night's events came flooding back to her and she systematically flicked through the pair's conversations in her head. As if she was in the middle of a huge computer, she downloaded all the information and deleted anything that was irrelevant. All the relevant information was now filed away in the cloud inside her brain ready to be typed up in her report that morning. First, she just needed to get past the headache encapsulating her brain.

Suddenly she remembered how much she had wanted Thomas to make a move with her. But he hadn't, and she was severely disappointed, although Bianca was sure that she didn't show it. *Thomas probably doesn't even know that I like him that way,* Bianca thought. She suddenly caught herself. *What was she thinking? She 'liked him' that way? She shouldn't be 'liking him' that way. He was a subject. Yes, she could kiss him. Yes, she could sleep with him, but no, she wasn't supposed to 'like him'.*

The kettle boiled and Bianca made herself an instant coffee. She wasn't a coffee snob that had to have coffee made from a machine. She actually quite enjoyed instant coffee, as long as it wasn't International Roast, in which case she probably would have preferred to drink horse piss.

Bianca sat down at her desk with the hot cup of the magical substance. It seemed to instantly make her headache feel better - or was that the two headache tablets she had taken? Her laptop lit up and she put on her librarian style reading glasses and started typing away, revealing the findings from studying her subject over the past couple of weeks, and in particular last night.

She had typed about three pages of information when she stopped. She had finished her coffee and felt like another one, but that wasn't why she stopped. Bianca had a thought: *I wonder why the clients want this type of information on the subjects?* Realistically, even the half-interesting stuff often seemed irrelevant in the bigger picture of the world. Yeah, there had been some interesting and obviously somewhat classified information revealed to her about weapons systems, which political leaders had a crack habit and the depths of the VICPOL corruption, but it wasn't as if she had ever had revealed to her the safe houses for the heads of the Islamic State in Australia, or where weapons of mass destruction were actually hidden, or that Barrack Obama was a Muslim, or a foreign alien, or both.

Bianca looked down at her empty coffee cup and thought she really must buy herself a set of bigger mugs, just as she had got the large wineglasses.

She reread her report. The only half-interesting piece of information she had managed to obtain was Thomas's involvement with the Sunrise Hotel Siege. The siege had taken place about three years ago, and the SOGGIES had been called in to deal with the situation as it was way beyond general duties and too much for CIT. Thomas was a Sergeant at the time and he was the Team Supervisor. Bianca already knew a lot of the information that Thomas told her, as it had been plastered across all media platforms for months following, but despite this she still put it in the report.

The two offenders were armed with sawn-off shot guns. They had entered the Sunrise Hotel located in the Melbourne CBD at 0855hrs on a Tuesday morning. They were fully clothed in black, including black balaclavas. Their original objective was to conduct an armed hold-up; however, this turned into a hostage situation when the offenders heard the police sirens prior to their demands being met, and had a chance to evade the authorities. In total, they were holding eighteen people, including staff, in the hotel lobby and adjoining areas, with an unknown number still in the hotel.

VICPOL initially evacuated the surrounding buildings, which quickly cascaded into an evacuation of the adjoining streets and a lock-down of the rest of the CBD. The SOG were dispatched and what went down was not according to the plan or any policing handbook. By the end of the siege, both offenders were dead, as well as seven civilians. It was a complete clusterfuck.

Bianca continued typing away. She was now onto the more interesting parts; things that she'd been told that she knew hadn't been for public consumption. This wasn't general knowledge or anything you could find on a search engine. This was the type of information the clients were after - so she had always been told.

She remembered Thomas drinking possibly even more than her. The alcohol definitely seemed to help let his censors down. He'd seemed quite willing to talk about his police career, and in particular the siege. She thought he probably liked talking to her about being in the SOG because he thought Bianca would be impressed by his former employment. She wasn't overly impressed by that, but what did impress her was his ability to put his ego momentarily aside and actually talk about his involvement and the decision making surrounding the siege, especially given the horrific outcome.

Her phone beeped. She looked at her device and it was Thomas. *'Thank u for last night. I had a gr8 time. I will be at the coffee shop this arv. Hope to see u X.'*

Bianca caught herself smiling. *Why was she so happy?* Bianca knew the answer to her own question, but decided to ignore that for the moment. She also noticed his shorthand text. *Laziness*, Bianca thought, but then again, every man she had met was a lazy prick in some shape or form. She texted back: *Thank you, so did I. I am busy today sorry, maybe another time.*

Inner Eastern Suburbs, Melbourne, Victoria

Thomas saw his private phone light up. He was happy she had replied so fast. He read Bianca's text and his heart sank. *'Maybe another time.' What the fuck? That was code for thanks, but no thanks. Surely he didn't get it that wrong?* She had come across as really quite interested in him. She had appeared happy and willing to hear him talk about the book and all his stress. He had even taken comfort in talking to her about the Sunrise Hotel siege, the event he was going to fictionalise just enough to allow it to play a major part in his book. *No*, he thought, *maybe she was just busy today.*

Thomas realised how disappointed he was and decided he was not going to give up that easily. He had felt the sexual tension and knew it wasn't just in his mind. There absolutely had been a huge amount of rapport between them. Last night he would have liked to take Bianca back to his 4WD, lay the seats down and ravage her; but he had thought it best to give it a bit more time, as he actually really liked her, he couldn't deny that.

'I would love to come see some of your art u told me about last night. Can I come to urs 1 night this week?' Thomas typed on his phone. He hit the send button. The text went flying through

the network and to her phone, never to be taken back.

Thomas felt almost sick. He so badly wanted her answer to be 'Yes', but maybe he was being delusional? *Maybe she was just a nice person – but why had she agreed to go out to dinner with me in the first place? Or maybe the offer of free wine was enough to convince her, since she had joked about being an alcoholic.*

After what seemed a lifetime, his phone lit up and it was Bianca. *Sure, you are welcome to come over on Sunday night, bring wine.* A big smile spread across Thomas's face. He looked like a child on Christmas morning with a shiny new bike sitting under the Christmas tree. *'Will do X'*, he texted back. He had noticed she didn't send any crosses or hugs or even smiley faces. He wasn't going to let that worry him, though. What was an emoji in the scheme of things? He had always been told 'good things come to those that wait, but greater things come to those that pursue.' He was glad he had pursued.

Thomas's heart was singing as he wrapped his body holster on and safety checked his Glock 22 before securing it inside its bed. His woollen pullover easily concealed the firearm, but it was cold enough outside to freeze a flat-breasted girl's tits off, so Thomas knew to be smart and wear his grey duffle jacket. He threw his laptop bag across his body and walked out the door. He needed to get into some of his therapy, but first he had some study to do.

CHAPTER 7

South Melbourne, Victoria

"WE RECEIVED YOUR PRELIMINARY report yesterday, Bianca, thank you. I have to say, though, it was just *preliminary*. I'm sure the client will be wanting to obtain more information than that. A whole heap of it was public knowledge. Realistically, you could have just googled it."

Bianca shuffled her feet. *Fuck me*, she thought, *Cheryl was a bitch sometimes!*

"Cheryl, as always, I have just delivered what was relayed to me. There was a whole heap of other boring shit he talked about, but I can assure you that was of no interest. I thought I actually did okay considering the time frame I've worked within."

Cheryl looked at Bianca, and Bianca could tell that she didn't seem to be buying it. Bianca continued, "Did you see where he started to tell me about the choice of weapons and entry tactics his SOG team used for the soup sandwich? It was essentially his decision, you know? He was leading the team. There was liaison with the SOG Commander and the Team Manager, but basically they put the main tactical decisions in his hands.

He reckoned they knew it might all go to shit and didn't want the blame. After the deaths of so many hostages, Thomas was pulled through the absolute wringer for it. Amongst all the political games that went on, he ended up with a promotion, but that was actually a demotion in his opinion. He was made a Team Manager in the SOG, which meant he basically became a paper pusher. No more field action for him. He couldn't stand the paperwork so he left, but the fact is he was indirectly pushed out. Did you not read that? That's gold. Surely the client will be happy with that information?" Bianca caught her breath, hoping that her dog and pony show had sounded convincing.

"Yes, I did read all that, Bianca. I always read everything in your reports. There was some interesting information that you did obtain." Cheryl knew how to manipulate her. The years of study had shown that the woman responded to being criticised, then being praised, then being presented with a challenge or criticised again. It was almost the opposite of the 'Critical Feedback Sandwich'. She was always wanting to prove herself, show how good she was. Like most of the Agency's subjects, she was so vain and self-absorbed, it was all about Bianca. *Worse than Queen Victoria*, Cheryl often thought.

"I just feel there is more information to be obtained from this subject. We want to give the client as much as we can." Cheryl took a sip from her water bottle. She always seemed to be drinking water. The woman was like a camel. Bianca thought that if she drank water like that she would never get off the toilet.

"That's fine," Bianca answered, happy to have already agreed to Thomas coming to see her on Sunday. She would have been pissed off if Cheryl had said she'd obtained enough information and to disappear out of his life just as quickly as she had entered it. Bianca took a seat.

She thought how horny she was right now. The sexual tension at the table during their dinner had been so thick and Bianca had sat there wet for the most part of the night. She thought about how good Thomas had looked and how she had caught him looking at her too.

I know he wants it, she thought to herself, sending tingles down her body. Bianca squirmed in the seat.

"Everything okay?" asked David who had walked in halfway through Bianca's briefing. "I mean, you look like you need Combantrin or something."

Bianca didn't particularly like David. In her opinion he was an obsequious nerdy pervert who had no clue about any type of field operation, yet somehow he had the title of Ops Manager. She swore that all he did was sit in and listen to Bianca's briefings and walk in on her wellness checks at the most opportunistic time he could.

"My arse is fine, thank you very much."

"Oh, we all know that, Bianca," David said, winking at Cheryl. He thought his boss might like that joke.

"Yes, we all know how fantastic Bianca's arse is." Cheryl agreed, looking at her two subordinates. "Bianca just needs to use it a bit more with her subject I think."

"I haven't got there yet, Cheryl. He has been very open with me with just my initial situational manipulation. I think he actually may really *like* me."

"Don't flatter yourself," Cheryl snapped. She continued, "Or worse, fall for him. What would we do with you then?" Cheryl raised her perfect eyebrow at her. Bianca wondered how Cheryl's perfect brows could still rise in such a way, considering that she knew the woman had a face full of the Iraqi weapon.

"Chances of that, zero," Bianca replied lying.

"I should think so. You know better than to get involved emotionally with a subject. You've been doing this for long enough now."

David was sitting at the meeting table, tapping away on his Surface Pro. Bianca wondered if the man actually did any productive work. All her jobs seemed to come directly from Cheryl. She knew there was admin support, but she didn't have anything to do with them. They just data entered, managed employee timesheets and client confidentiality, that type of thing. The type of thing that really didn't interest Bianca.

"Bianca is due for her wellness check," David piped up, reminding Cheryl as if she didn't know.

Cheryl knew. She always knew when her subjects were due. The routine wellness check was a vital part of the study. She had to show how they would put up with being subjected, over and over again, all in the name of their work. It was of course for The Agency, in the name of something else.

Bianca wanted to tell David to fuck off, but she knew to keep her mouth shut. Anyway, she looked smoking, just as Cheryl wanted her to. Bianca admitted to herself that she had struggled more than usual to lose the extra body fat. She knew the big bowl of carbs from the night out with her subject and all the wine she had engulfed lately hadn't helped either. Despite this, two hours of lapping and exhausting sessions on her rowing machine every day had got her within reach of the required target.

"Get yourself in the examination room, Bianca. We better check that arse of yours." Cheryl winked at David. He smiled. He knew what Cheryl was up to.

"Is her arse okay?"

"Felt just fine to me. Thomas should have fun with it." Cheryl reported to David. David stopped for a moment, picturing Thomas bending Bianca over.

"Lucky fucker," he said under his breath.

"What was that?" Cheryl asked raising her head from the keyboard, where she had started entering Bianca's physiological and emotional responses from the wellness check for David's collation and interpretation.

"Nothing, I was just daydreaming."

"She has a fair bit of work to do, you know. She hasn't even bedded him yet. I told her he might be difficult for her."

"But not difficult for you though, was it?" David asked with a knowing smile on his face.

"Correct. How else do you think I convinced him to join The Agency? He thought he was too good for us. Vain prick."

Cheryl shivered. *Why was the air-conditioning even on?* She asked herself. *It was something like 12 degrees outside.* Cheryl continued, "Some aren't as easy to recruit as Bianca was. All we had to do was make her feel that she was specially chosen, she was somebody. Oh, and give her a choice of firearm. That helped too."

"I thought she was specially chosen?" David asked questioning.

"It was more a bit of good luck on the Agency's behalf. The Department highlighted her as a potential subject, and they picked perfectly. We just feed her ego and she does as we want when we want; but you know that, you finalise the data."

"Yes, she has been a great subject. She is so consistent and her pretexting skills exceptional, proof of how we can engineer."

"That she has, but she has a challenge with Thomas. As we know, the man is way too loose for his own good, but he is our best-looking male subject. What happens in the next few days should be *very* interesting." Cheryl emptied her water bottle and put it down on the desk. She walked out of the office and to the main area where the administration team were.

"Can someone do something about that air conditioning? If I'd wanted to work in fucking Antarctica I would have taken a posting with that division!"

City Fringe, Melbourne, Victoria

T HOMAS ENTERED THE PUBLIC bar. It was a bit of a trendy looking joint, as the majority of pubs now were. Even most of the dives in Melbourne had been renovated to some point - they just couldn't survive otherwise.

Fucking hipsters, Thomas thought. *It's all your fault. Whatever happened to men being men and being able to drink a Victorian Bitter? But no, a VB wasn't good enough now. You needed to have some pale ale from a local microbrewery on tap just to capture an audience.* Thomas caught his thoughts. At one stage he had thought that he was the blueprint for manliness, but now he too was finding that he had given in to the world of food, wine and fashion that seemed to epitomise Melbourne. *Well, at least I have some facial hair*, he thought. Then he swore in his head as he realised that a beard was now a hipster thing to have. *As long as I don't get wide-rimmed glasses, I'll be okay.*

He took a seat in a booth and placed his midi of VB in front of him. He pretended to be looking at the racing form guide.

Just looking at the front cover was an effort as he loathed horses. Gary Stephenson, his latest subject, was only a few metres away and within earshot. He was talking with another barfly. They seemed to be discussing the TOTE and the racing taking place at Pakenham and Caulfield that day.

"She's a Rose - that filly is a sure thing," the unknown barfly said to Gary. "Three wins from three starts, she is on fire!"

"Nothing's a sure thing in this game," Gary replied to his mate. "For Caulfield, my money is on Sky Alight."

This was Thomas's second time in the bar that Gary seemed to like. The man seemed to like many things: horses, pokies, beer and even cigarettes. Thomas was shocked that anyone still even smoked these days. Gary made Thomas feel better about his own shortcomings.

Thomas decided to make a move. "Hey, I heard you say She's a Rose is a sure thing. You reckon she's in with a good chance, then?"

The men looked at Thomas, who was now standing at the bar with them. The barmaid looked up momentarily at the men then returned to wiping over the top shelf bottles of alcohol sitting precariously on the shelf.

"Huh, if you wanna listen to this joker, then yeah she's a sure thing!" Gary said, laughing at the insult directed at his barfly mate.

"Well the track was a heavy eight, but it'll dry out a bit today so it'll suit her. She's good on a medium to heavy track," the bar fly retaliated. He seemed pleased with being able to pass on such valuable knowledge.

"Thanks," Thomas said. "I think I'll bet on her, then."

"Hey, you were in here the other day weren't you? I hadn't seen you before that. We know all the regulars in this joint." Gary took a gulp of his schooner of beer. It was also a VB.

"Yeah I was. My local has gone all upmarket, you know, with a change in management. Two poofters are now running it. I'm looking for a new watering hole."

"Don't blame ya. Well, this one is still okay. They did some renos on it about a year ago, but they kept the VB and the raffle girls. Thank fuck."

The men laughed and Thomas joined them in downing about a quarter of their beers in one hit.

"You going to stay for the raffle and tits?"

Thomas paused for a moment. He would like to, but he thought best not to overstay his welcome at the local heavy pub. Plus, he thought he probably wouldn't get much out of Gary with the girls around. Too much of a distraction for them both, actually. He was happy to have just built some initial rapport.

"Nah, I'd like to, but I've got to work later this arv."

"Well you miss out, I tell you. There'll be some nice arse walking around."

"Yeah that would have been good, my old pub is lucky to even get a girl walk in, even one that's clothed!" Thomas exclaimed.

"They get good ones in here, top shelf. If you'd started coming here a few years ago, then you would know what I'm on about. There was this one girl that used to come, she only came for a short time but my God her tits were like perfect coconuts! Real, too!"

Thomas smiled. It never ceased to amaze him how men always thought girl's breasts were real. If someone wanted to believe something was real, then all they did was convince themselves it was. *Just like Santa Claus,* he thought, *or religion in general.*

Bianca wondered what the fuck Thomas was doing at a pub at that time of the morning. *Maybe he has a gambling addiction?* she thought. *Maybe he actually has PTSD and has resorted to the pokies.* Bianca felt actual sadness for a moment and The Whitlams' song *Blow up the Pokies* came into her head. *Yep, that's what they should do, blow all the fucking things up. But no, the government would never ban the pokies, they wanted all the money. Tell us all that the money is being used to build infrastructure, such a load of spin. Just another way they screw over their own citizens,* she thought.

She was sitting across the other side of the road with her hair all tucked up into a baseball cap and her big designer sunnies on. She had on her Lorna Jane leggings, merino wool long-sleeved top and puffer vest. She had a jogger pram with the shade cover pulled completely over so the inside of the pram was not visible. Bianca was satisfied that she looked like every other trendy mum who was trying to lose weight at the same time as eating their Persian love cake and drinking soy lattes. Her head was buried in the latest issue of *Australian Vogue,* or so it appeared.

Thomas stayed in the pub until just before lunch, then made his way back to his Range Rover which was perfectly parallel parked. Bianca stayed where she was, but watched him the whole time, gently rocking the baby-less pram back and forth. She had read the pub's outside blackboard that stated there would be titty girls and raffles in the public bar from 2pm to 6pm, and was surprised Thomas had left before copping an eyeful.

Bianca sat in place for another fifteen minutes before finishing her magazine. The late morning sun had been a welcome change from the rain and wind that had inundated Melbourne over the past weeks. She thought his visit to the pub at that time of the day had been odd, and the pub wasn't exactly near his favourite coffee spot either. She had, of course, followed him. She knew where he lived, as that was part of the basic information provided to her in the job file. She would never go to a subject's house; well, not without being invited. She had waited in her car in a carpark on the corner of a street leading out onto a main road that Thomas had to take. Anyone living in his or the surrounding streets would end up driving along the street to turn onto the main road if they wanted to get anywhere in Melbourne. She was pleased with herself for not missing his car as it stopped at the t–intersection. It was a white Range Rover so at least it wasn't too inconspicuous, not like a silver Commodore or something.

Bianca thought that Thomas's car was much like himself. Though it wasn't outlandish it still demanded attention and it looked hot. She wondered how he could afford such a luxury car, especially with a mortgage, wife and a couple of kids.

He must be drowning in debt and he is apparently retired. He must have another job, Bianca concluded. However, there was nothing about another job mentioned in Thomas's file that had been provided to her.

Bianca drove a black Volkswagen Golf. Given her RAAF compensation payout, she could have afforded an Audi or a Lexus, but she was more practical than that. She had better things to spend her money on, like leather jackets and designer shoes.

She drove back to the favourite coffee shop. She spotted Thomas's car pulled up a street away from the café. He usually parked closer, but the streets were even busier than usual and Bianca guessed the nice weather had brought everyone out for the day.

Bianca didn't need to see any more. She just wanted confirmation that he had returned to his favourite spot to undertake his flirting, coffee drinking, and possibly some writing.

She couldn't help but think that the pub was so strange. What was even stranger, was that it was a pub she was familiar with. She had wished she had been able to walk in or even look in through the windows to see what he was actually doing in there, but of course she would never have compromised herself like that. Even sitting across the road in her 'disguise' was a little risky, but it had worked for her in the past so best to stick with something that had been proven.

Thomas had been at the pub without his laptop bag slung across him, so Bianca knew he wasn't doing any writing in there. *That environment surely wasn't conducive for artistic expression? Well maybe he was having a drink, stimulation for his artistic expression,* she thought. The famous words of Ernest Hemingway entered her mind: *"Write drunk, edit sober".* She smiled at the thought. However, she still felt a little uneasy about the fact she didn't know why he was there. But the thing that bothered her the most was that *she* didn't need to go to the pub. There was actually no reason for her to be there at all. Bianca had his phone number and she knew she just had to go the coffee shop between certain times and he would almost definitely be there. The guy was even coming around to her place on Sunday evening! She couldn't help but ask herself why she felt the need to start stalking him in this way.

Bianca answered her own question. She had followed her gut. There was something that Cheryl had said that Bianca hadn't been able to shake. *"This one is different."* Those words of Cheryl's kept resonating inside her head. Bianca needed to find out what made this subject so different and now his visit to the pub had only increased her curiosity.

We love because he first loved us

John 4:19

CHAPTER 9

Outer Eastern Suburbs, Melbourne, Victoria

B IANCA'S INTERCOM BUZZED. S HE had a look at the screen and could see it was Thomas.

"Come on up," she said into the speaker and pressed the button to release the front doors of the apartment building.

Bianca unlocked and opened her own front door. Thomas was there holding two bottles of wine. One red and one white. She looked at the bottles.

Thomas noticed her scrutinising his gifts. "I wasn't sure which one to get so I just got both," he laughed. Bianca smiled, she was happy he had brought both.

"Come on in, it's good to see you." She leant in and kissed Thomas on the cheek. Instantly there were tingles down her body and Bianca quickly pulled away. *Fuck this feeling*, she thought. *Why was this happening, and with a subject?*

Samson came over to Thomas and starting wrapping himself in and out of his legs, rubbing himself up against his ankles as he manoeuvred in figure-of-eights. His tail was high and proud. Thomas didn't particularly like cats, but then he had never had much to do with them. He thought they looked so smug and as if they were going to rip you a new one at any point in time if they wanted to.

"Samson likes you," Bianca commented. "You're lucky, because if my cat thinks you're an arsehole then you probably are."

Thomas momentarily pondered on this and thought himself lucky. He gave the cat a pat on its back. *Better keep on the good side of that one*, was the thought that crossed his mind.

"Make yourself at home. I 'll get some wineglasses." Bianca whisked herself away and left Thomas standing in the living area with Samson, who still seemed to enjoy rubbing his fur onto Thomas's chino pants.

Thomas looked around the apartment. It wasn't huge, but it was spacious and very light. All the walls were a shade of white with light floorboards and light coloured blinds. There was minimal furniture, but it still somehow felt cosy. He thought that had something to do with her use of soft furnishings, especially on the couch and floor. The electric fire also helped. It had that real Scandinavian feel, almost like something out of an IKEA catalogue, but a bit more upmarket. Paintings and charcoal drawings adorned the walls. All positioned perfectly and not competing against each other.

One particular painting caught his attention. He stepped back and looked it up and down, like some type of art critic. Thomas thought it was really interesting and pleasing to the eye, but he couldn't make out exactly what the painting was. He stepped back in again to take a closer look.

Bianca entered the room with two large wine glasses in her hand. Thomas thought they were extraordinarily huge, and wondered if Bianca had accidently mistaken a pet store for Myer.

She saw Thomas looking at the painting intently. Bianca spoke, "Some subjects shouldn't be studied. Sometimes it's best not to try to work them out."

Thomas's stare was suddenly redirected to her. She had placed the glasses on the coffee table and was pouring the sauvignon blanc into them. She filled the aquarium-like glasses three-quarters of the way up, basically emptying the bottle of wine. Bianca then made herself comfortable on the couch, tucking her feet up in towards her legs on the couch. She seemed oblivious to what she had just said, and more interested in her feline friend who had suddenly jumped up into her lap.

"I'm just a bit taken with that painting, it intrigues me," Thomas said, stepping away from the artwork and taking a seat on the couch next to Bianca and Samson.

"Glad you like it, it's one of my favourite pieces. It's so representative of me."

"Because it's beautiful?" Thomas asked in an attempt at flattery.

"No, because it's a big mess."

Thomas was silent for a moment, then he laughed. He had got her joke. Well he thought it was a joke, he never could be too sure. He felt as though some chapters in the *Book of*

· 67 ·

Bianca were so hard to read, yet others were like story-time on *Play School*.

He looked at her for a smile but there was no smile, just a wineglass on her pink lips. Her lips were full and she had on a rosy pink lip stain. He wondered what they felt like and hoped it wouldn't be long before he found out.

"What's that pendant on your necklace?" Thomas leant in and picked up the cameo pendant while sweeping his fingers across Bianca's décolletage. Thomas's face was right in near Bianca's chest and he could see her rise and fall. "Is that an angel?"

He really hoped it wasn't. He didn't want to find out now that she was some sort of religious freak and there would be no chance of finding out what any of her lips tasted like. *Shit, she is Italian*, he thought. *She's Catholic for sure.*

"No," Bianca replied. "It's Diana the Huntress." Thomas just stared at her blankly. "Okay, you obviously haven't heard of her."

He nodded in agreement.

"Well, Diana was a goddess in the times of Italian Neopaganism and Stregheria. She was able to talk to the animals and she was one of the three maiden goddesses who swore never to marry."

"So I'm guessing you relate to her then, being an animal lover and never marrying?"

"Kinda, except Diana was a virgin." Bianca smiled a smile at Thomas that said: "And of course I'm not."

Thomas read the smile and smiled back. He was liking where this was going.

"Oh, and yes Diana was an animal lover..." Bianca paused. "But she was also a hunter; despite her feelings, she still killed." Bianca suddenly got up and Samson sprang off her lap. "Shit, I almost forgot the lasagne, I hope it's not burnt."

"I thought I could smell something," Thomas said without thinking. Bianca glared at him. He quickly made an attempt at recovery, "And it smells lovely." Bianca smiled and raced into the kitchen to save her dish.

After finishing off over half a baking tray of the traditional meal, the pair retired back to the couch. Thomas noticed that Samson was fast asleep on an armchair. *What a life that cat has. He does whatever he wants and I reckon he has her wrapped around his little paw.* Thomas realised he was jealous of a cat. *Idiot*, he thought to himself shaking his head.

Another bottle of wine was opened and Thomas filled up their glasses in the same manner as Bianca had previously.

Bianca snuggled in a little. Thomas noticed how she seemed completely at ease, and he too felt relaxed.

"Thomas, I have a bit of a question to ask you."

He looked into her eyes. "Sure, shoot away."

"You said you are retired, but you're not that much older than me. I was just wondering how you could still afford everything. I mean surely you still have a mortgage, plus your wife and kids and all the other bits and pieces of everyday life. I saw your four-wheel drive the other night after dinner and that's certainly not a cheap car either. I mean I don't mean to be nosey, but I was just wondering...?"

Thomas deliberated on her question. He had the answer. It

was the same answer he told his wife, his family and anyone else that asked. He decided not to answer her straight up. He was going to counter-question. He actually had the same question for her.

"Funny you ask me that, because I was wondering the same thing about you. I mean surely you don't sell enough artwork per month to afford all this." Thomas waved his hand around the apartment. "I also have seen your taste in handbags and shoes."

Bianca took a sip of her wine. She was surprised he had counter-questioned her, but of course she had a cover story.

"Well that's absolutely a fair enough question. I actually do sell a bit of my work."

Thomas was surprised and it showed on his face.

"You look surprised. My work is unique and quite in demand."

Thomas lowered his head. He felt ashamed and thought he was now back on the bottom rung of Bianca's ladder for questioning her talent.

She continued, "In saying that, however, I do freelance work at a number of fine art galleries. I specialise in art curation. I help them with their exhibitions etc."

Hearing this made Thomas feel a bit better. He had another sip of his wine and watched as Bianca got up and shuffled the music on the iPod that was docked. He thought she sure had a wide musical taste. Since he had been there he had heard everything from Taylor Swift to Tool. Just no Adele.

Bianca sat back down and once again tucked up her feet. This time her feet were touching Thomas's legs. Thomas noticed this subtle come-on straight away.

"You didn't answer my question."

"What question was that?" asked Thomas, pretending to act stupid.

"About your retirement? I mean if you have a money tree planted out the back you could have at least brought me some seeds..." Bianca laughed and continued, "Hey, if you are growing cannabis and dealing it, I won't tell anyone ... each to their own."

Thomas laughed at Bianca even considering he might be dealing drugs. "Definitely not. I am retired from the police, but I do work another job and it does not involve prohibited substances."

"Oh well, that makes sense then. What do you do?"

"I'm head of security at a large company."

Bianca had to stop herself from spitting out her wine all over his white t-shirt. The look on her face was of utter disgust. Thomas couldn't help but notice it.

"Everything all right - is the wine all right?"

"The wine is just fine," Bianca snapped. "It's just, I mean, a security guard? Really?" She looked as if she wanted to vomit.

Thomas didn't know what to say. *What was wrong with being a security guard?* he thought. Actually, he knew the answer to that question. He remembered the disdain he had for private security personnel when he was with VICPOL.

Thomas retaliated, "I'm not a security guard, Bianca. I'm head of the security for the whole company. I'm in charge of all the guards and the facility in general. It's an important job." Thomas could hear the desperation in his voice. He was shocked at how much he wanted to impress the woman. He also was surprised she was so unimpressed by his chosen fake employment. He had thought it was a good cover and no one had given him shit about it before. *Why am I so desperate to impress you?* he asked Bianca in his own head. Sure, she was hot and she may not be a hairdresser, but still it wasn't as if she had the most riveting job herself. Art curation? Come on, yawn.

CHAPTER 10

Outer Eastern Suburbs, Melbourne, Victoria

B IANCA WAS NOT HAPPY with this newly acquired information. She still liked the guy, but now he had fallen off the pedestal that Bianca had unintentionally put him on inside her head. Her reaction was even a surprise to herself.

"Oh I'm sure it is an important job," Bianca said, sounding bored. Thinking about sitting around in a security office all night secretly hoping that something actually might happen, well that sounded like the most boring thing in the world to her.

Thomas heard the boredom in her voice. He couldn't believe that he may have screwed up his chances with the girl just because she thought his job was incongruous to her perception of him. Most women wouldn't have cared about that; they were usually more concerned with the money being in the bank rather than how it had been obtained.

Bianca got up off the couch and her feet left Thomas's leg. Her eyes zeroed in on him. "I'm going to go get a Panadol, I can feel a headache coming on." She walked out of the living area leaving Thomas alone with the cat. Samson looked at Thomas in disgust, jumped down from the armchair and proceeded to follow Bianca out of the room.

Damn cat, Thomas thought, *it even thinks it is better than me.* He didn't like the feeling, the feeling that someone thought they were better than him. Even after the siege mess, he still felt that he was an impressive person. That feeling had taken a while to regain, but he did get it back. He knew that that particular incident was never actually his fault solely, so why should he feel bad about it? He had come to the conclusion that sometimes things just don't go to plan. He had decided when he was recruited by The Agency that he wouldn't let that one event in his life define him. Prior to the siege, he had had what most would describe as a prestigious career with VICPOL. The Agency had told him that he was "an exceptional operator who had displayed courage even through the storm". They continued to tell him that his involvement in that incident wasn't enough for them not to want him to work for them; quite to the contrary, those involved in high stress situations often made the best operators. That was if they didn't succumb to the mental health plague that seemed to be out of control. He smiled at himself, suddenly feeling better. *Yes, he had no mental health issues. He was exceptional, he just needed Bianca to think that.*

She appeared back in the living room with Samson on her

heels. He was licking around his little milk-stained mouth. *Fuck me*, Thomas thought, *that cat is spoiled. I bet it sleeps on the bed with her.* Thomas found himself once again jealous of the cat, wishing he was Samson.

Bianca walked straight past Thomas on the couch and sat down on the single armchair where the cat had previously been sleeping. Thomas noticed her change in demeanour towards him and he knew he had to do something if he wanted to take Samson's place in the bed with her.

"I'm sorry Bianca, but I've actually been lying to you." Thomas's eyes now looked like Samson's would have if Samson was a puppy dog.

Bianca put down her wineglass on the coffee table, looked at him and said, "Well you are a guy, so that's to be expected."

Touché, Thomas thought. *She must really have dated some cockheads.* He continued, "I lied to you about my work. I'm not a security guard."

"Yeah you told me that, you are *head* of security, very important job, remember?" Bianca stated, sounding facetious.

"No, I don't do that job at all."

Bianca raised her eyebrows as much as her muscles would allow. Now this was an interesting change in events and she wondered what the bloke actually did for a living.

"Well thank fuck for that, but why would you lie to me?" Another big gulp of wine went down her throat and into her bloodstream.

Thomas didn't say anything. Instead he picked up his wine glass and followed suit in taking a couple of big swigs from it before placing it back on the beech lamp table next to him. He finally answered, "I *had* to."

"You didn't *have* to, Thomas," Bianca hissed. "You don't *have* to do anything." He thought she sounded pissed off with being lied to. Inside, though, she was secretly happy that the security job was a lie; but she was dying to know what other work he did.

"Yeah I did. I've actually never told anyone this because I'm not supposed to, I mean even my wife doesn't know!"

Wow, Bianca thought, *if this is true then this is huge.* She noticed Thomas was sounding a bit nervous. She read his body language and it appeared as though he was actually telling the truth.

"Your wife doesn't even know?" repeated Bianca. "Well I think you're playing with fire there. What are you? Some type of contract killer or something?" Bianca asked, laughing. She stopped laughing for a second and wondered whether her Beretta was locked in its case or sitting under her bed ready to go. If he actually was some type of mercenary she might suddenly be needing it. She started laughing again at her own ridiculous thought.

"No not a contract killer, but just as secretive." Thomas took a drink from his wine. He had chosen well, it was a smooth drop. He thought for a moment how he felt like James Bond in one of his movies, except he didn't have a martini, a tuxedo or even his sidearm for that matter.

What in the world did he do? wondered Bianca. *Secretive? He must work for ASIO, but then if he had worked for them there was no way The Agency would have taken on the job, surely?* She then had another thought: *maybe The Agency didn't even know he worked for ASIO? No, no way, they would definitely know that type of information.*

Bianca was very intrigued now. She thought this must be the information the client was after, not information about the Sunrise Hotel siege at all. She was smiling and pleased with her own blagging abilities. She decided then to reward Thomas for telling her his secret. However, he hadn't told her everything just yet so she needed to give him some more motivation.

She came back over to the couch that Thomas was on and sat on his lap holding her wine. She pressed her backside down into him. Thomas was staring into her eyes and he immediately wrapped an arm around her waist. The man was looking very pleased with himself.

Thomas noticed how Bianca's mood and behaviour towards him had changed in an instant. She seemed very happy now and impressed by the fact that he wasn't a security guard and even more impressed that he did something secretive. Now she was on his lap and hanging onto his every word.

"Well, Thomas, you are making me feel very special, choosing me to tell," Bianca said, looking straight into her subject's light blue eyes and fluttering her own brown version.

"I've never told anyone, but I want to tell you - I think I *need* to tell you." Thomas couldn't believe the words that were falling out of his mouth. He had never considered telling anyone despite wanting to; and this certainly hadn't been part of his plan for tonight, but he just so desperately wanted this woman to be impressed by him.

Can't have her thinking I'm a loser security guard, when I am actually so much more than that, he thought to himself.

"You really are making me feel privileged. I mean, aren't you afraid I might tell someone?" Bianca pushed herself down onto him harder, hence making the man harder.

Thomas admired Bianca positioned there. She sure looked good sitting on his lap. She felt good too, her skin was soft, but her body toned. His penis was hard for her and he thought she must be able to feel it through their clothes. He looked back into her eyes. They didn't look as if they belonged to Jezebel. They were more like Joan of Arc eyes.

"No, I trust you. Plus, even if you did there's no proof of The Agency's existence. They have a front and they cover their tracks."

Bianca almost choked on her own tongue. *The Agency? Did she just hear that? No, she must have heard wrong. She had to have heard wrong.*

"The Agency?" Bianca asked shifting the weight of her bony backside from one arse cheek to another. She couldn't help but notice that Thomas's hand had partially gone up under her white singlet top and he was gently touching her back and sweeping his fingers across her stomach and back around again.

"Yeah, that's where I work. They pay me to obtain information from people."

Holy shit, thought Bianca, *What the fuck is going on?* She had to maintain her cool. *Can't give anything away,* she thought. She needed to play the game as if she didn't know what game he was playing, that is, if he was actually even playing one.

"*So* you are like a spy then," she asked, trying to sound very impressed.

"Exactly," answered Thomas as he took another drink from his wine and explored Bianca further with the other hand.

Fuck me, Bianca thought. *Cheryl would have kittens if she heard one of her employees refer to themselves as a spy. If he did work for The Agency, then he is a hopeless operator, way too arrogant for his own good. Or maybe he is the exact opposite: if he knows who I really am, then he is an exceptional operator.* If that was the case, Bianca knew she had been played.

Bianca caught her thoughts. Though she had no idea what was going on with Thomas being an Agency employee too, she suddenly realised how much more intriguing he now was. In fact, everything about this situation was now very intriguing. Thomas was somehow, and oddly, climbing his way back up onto her cognitive pedestal. She put her glass down and repositioned herself on Thomas so she was straddling him. She put her face in close to his and thought how good he smelt.

"Well you are a sexy spy. Your little secret is safe with me. I won't tell anyone." Bianca put her lips on his and the two started kissing passionately. The next thing Thomas had his hands up on Bianca's breasts and was grabbing at them. Bianca took Thomas's shirt off, baring his muscular chest. *He doesn't wax, thank God,* she thought, but not that he needed to, he had been blessed not to resemble King Kong.

Bianca suddenly got up off Thomas. The man looked like a devastated hot mess. "Where are you going?" he asked.

"To bed," she replied.

Thomas looked absolutely shattered. *What had just happened?* He thought to himself. *Surely she wouldn't leave me hanging?*

"You coming?" She smiled at him and held out her hand. Thomas couldn't remember a moment in his life that had been sexier.

He put his hand in hers and he let her lead him down the hall to her bedroom. He was surprised by his lack of stress given the fact he had just told her his big secret. In fact, he wasn't stressed at all. He actually felt better for telling her. She seemed impressed by him and it also appeared that she felt special that he had chosen her to be the one to tell.

Just make a woman feel special and they'll do whatever you want, he had once been told. Those words rung in his head.

"You know what your name should be?" Thomas said to Bianca as they entered the bedroom.

She didn't get a chance to answer before Thomas continued, "Biancaneve."

"Snow White?" Bianca questioned. "Why Snow White?"

"Because she was the fairest of them all."

Bianca looked at him, thinking that he actually looked like the fairest of them all. She was also very impressed with his use of Italian and wondered how long it had taken him to come up with that compliment. She fell onto her knees in front of him, looked up and spoke: "That's a beautiful compliment, I'd better thank you then."

CHAPTER 11

Domestic Terminal, Melbourne Airport, Victoria

WTF? WHY AM I *studying one of our own?* was all the text read. Cheryl looked at David. "Looks like Thomas has told her."

David shook his head. "Told you he was a loose cannon. This just proves it. The bloke is unbelievable. He'll say anything to get into a girl's pants and to big-note himself. He is fucking writing a book too. Imagine the shit he's written in there. I know he says it's all based around his VICPOL days, but I reckon something that resembles The Agency will be in there for sure, he is so conceited and he wouldn't be able to help it."

Cheryl just smiled. "It's Bianca, David. We know through the other subjects' reports that he has never revealed that level of information before, and he's been with us for over a year now. He has something for her, more than just sexual, I think."

"More than sexual? Well that would be unusual for him. What's the next move with Bianca? She is going to be pissed."

"We will tell Bianca that we got her to conduct an internal study. We'll say to her we had our concerns about Thomas's ability to be covert and keep his mouth shut about his job. As we know from all the studies on her, she loves feeling important and she is a fucking over-achiever. She will be thrilled that we chose her to conduct this study. She'll walk out the door with a head the size of Thomas's nuts by end of the briefing."

"Thomas's nuts hey?" David asked, looking at Cheryl with a smile.

"Yes, they are pretty huge."

The smile on David's face suddenly dropped. "Cheryl, so you truly believe Thomas has a thing for her?"

"Definitely."

"Well, what if the feeling is *mutual*?"

Cheryl picked up her bottle of water and had a drink. The airport air conditioning dried her skin out and the last thing she needed was to actually start looking her age.

"For someone who has a PhD, that's a pretty stupid thing to say. You should know our girl better than that now. She's been studied for three years, David. We have zero data that would even lean towards that hypothesis. She's cold as ice."

"Ice can melt, Cheryl."

"Not Bianca, she's the fucking Ice Queen!"

"Much like yourself." Cheryl glared at David. David looked away, thinking maybe he shouldn't have said that. He did need to remember he was on a lower pay tier than his boss.

"I'm going to text back to her and get her to come in tomorrow, since we're getting on our flight soon. We'll explain everything to her then."

"Everything?" David asked looking concerned.

"Of course not everything!" Sometimes Cheryl just couldn't believe that for someone so smart, he often asked the most stupid questions. "Just what we want her to know, and to do. I think we'll have some very interesting findings to present to the Department." Cheryl looked pleased and took another drink from her water bottle.

David also looked pleased. If this played out as Cheryl believed it would, then the past years of study would be worth it. With the new government, there had been talk about shutting The Agency down, that it wasn't financially feasible. *This, though,* thought David, *certainly might make the big wigs in Canberra sit up and pay attention.*

Outer Eastern Suburbs, Melbourne, Victoria

What was taking so long? Why hadn't Cheryl texted back yet? Bianca walked back into her bedroom with her freshly made coffee. Her white sheets were spread in different directions across the bed and her decorative cushions were on the floor along with her and Thomas's clothes. The sunlight was beaming in through the partially open blinds and the light was landing on Thomas's body as it spread across the bed like Jesus on the cross. The room smelt like sex.

Thomas suddenly moved in the bed. Bianca checked that her work phone was on silent and put it on the concealed shelf under the bed alongside her pistol. She got back into bed, propping herself up so she could drink her coffee.

"Morning, Beautiful." Thomas smiled at her. She had obviously woken him up when she was working her way back into bed.

"Morning."

Bianca looked at him. He looked perfect, as if he had had a full twelve hours sleep, instead of a night filled with hair grabbing, arse licking and her screaming her lungs out. She suddenly realised she was probably lucky the neighbours didn't call the cops.

"You want a coffee?" Bianca asked, being polite.

"No, not yet. I'm still waking up."

"By the looks of it, something is already wide awake." Bianca's eyes were on his penis which was standing at attention.

Thomas looked down at himself. "Oh that, that's a piss fat," he replied. "I better go to the bathroom."

The man got up and made his way into the ensuite and shut the door. Bianca quickly grabbed her phone. A message had come through. It was Cheryl: *Your appointment is scheduled for 1230hrs tomorrow.*

Tomorrow! Unbelievable. She would have to wait a whole day to find out what the hell was going on. Bianca looked at the time. *Fuck, it was already 10.15 am.* They had slept in! Bianca couldn't remember the last time she had slept in so late, but then she hadn't had such a physically and mentally draining night since being in the RAAF.

Thomas walked back into the bedroom, completely naked.

Bianca gently put her phone on the floor next to her for lack of a bedside table. She didn't have time to hide it, plus that would have looked suspicious.

"I was just checking the time, and its quarter past ten already. I have to go work at the gallery soon and I'm sure your wife will be wondering why you're not home yet." Bianca took a sip of her coffee.

"Shit, we slept in, didn't we? We must have exhausted each other," Thomas said with a cheeky smile, admiring Bianca's long legs half bent up on the bed as she sat perched drinking her morning brew. He thought how his wife never seemed to wake up looking so sexy, and he was surprised by his lack of usual momentary guilt.

"I am actually feeling pretty good," Bianca said, opening her legs just a touch. Thomas got the hint and came flying across the bed faster than Superman.

"I thought you needed to get ready for work?"

"I do, but I need you more." Bianca smiled with her brown eyes. Thomas felt himself harden up instantly, but he also felt something else. He realised that his feelings for this woman were running deeper than just lust. He felt that if he wasn't married, this was the type of woman he could wife.

The fact that Thomas was working for The Agency too had been at the forefront of her thoughts all the previous night and since she had awoken, but Bianca couldn't give this away. For all she knew, he might know she was an Agency employee too! She had decided to go with gut instinct and not say anything to him. During all her training that had been reinforced - to use your gut. No use revealing herself just in case he actually didn't know about her involvement. The same thought had kept crossing her mind: *if he did know about her, he was a good operator that's for sure, maybe even better than her.* It was all a mind fuck at the moment, but she was sure The Agency had a good reason and she would be fully briefed tomorrow. In the meantime she just needed to show patience and enjoy having Thomas's head buried between her legs.

CHAPTER 12

Somewhere in Canberra, Australian Capital Territory

"THANKS FOR COMING IN at such short notice."

"It's no problem, Michael. David and I were happy to come," replied Cheryl to her boss.

Michael continued, "As you are well aware, with the change in government, every departmental dollar is being scrutinised. They are asking questions of the feasibility and overall value of The Agency project."

Cheryl looked at David, who had frown lines on his face and his nose scrunched up. For a moment Cheryl thought he looked like a sewer rat.

"We are very much aware of the financial review of the Department and its projects. I think the Department needs to remind the Minister of the initial reason that The Agency was started. We are breaking new ground here. There has never been a study of its type conducted in Australia. We are almost four years in and I think the results speak for themselves!"

David butted in, "Yes, Michael, take Subject 003 for example..."

Michael interrupted, "003, what - the girl?"

"Yeah, the girl. The only female subject, actually. Bianca Beretta."

Michael laughed, "I'm sorry, that name just makes me laugh, she sounds like a porn star crossed with a Bond girl!" He continued to chuckle.

"Well, she kind of is."

Michael stopped laughing and looked at Cheryl and David. Cheryl hadn't changed a bit. She was still as beautiful and elegant as ever. However, he understood that her outside appearance wasn't a great representation of her inside. He knew first-hand of her clandestineness and how cunning she was. That's why he had put the former ASIS officer in charge of The Agency in the first place. David, on the other hand, looked exactly as he was. As much as he could be a pain in the arse, he was a great scientist and a real asset to the Department.

"In all seriousness, I have full knowledge of the findings from Subject 003. I read all the reports - I'm the one that fucking presents the findings to Canberra. That's why you guys are here. It's my head on the chopping block too, not just yours!"

Cheryl had been quiet, computing the conversation. She didn't want them to close down her baby. She was proud of what she had achieved since the instalment of the project and in her opinion there was still work to be done.

She finally spoke: "Subject 003 has been the greatest example of social engineering thus far. She is the epitome of proving how someone who has been exposed to trauma and extreme stress can be moulded into anyone we want her to be. For the most part, she takes orders without question. She presents no signs of humiliation, despite being continually subjected to our routine 'wellness checks' and unreasonable requests. She appears to have no concern for anything but pleasing The Agency, all so that she feels good about herself. Her own narcissism makes her an invaluable asset. Findings show that she has never ever revealed anything about the Agency or for that matter, hardly anything about herself to any of the other subjects who have studied her. She, on the other hand, usually always gets some info on our subjects' former lives out of them." Cheryl took a breath and sip of the coffee that had been made for her. She continued, "She's the model citizen. We know it's all about control, how we can control them. Bianca is proof of how the government can control people, especially if they have previously been subject to extreme stress or trauma. She has been absolute putty in our hands."

"We believe the fact she is female has increased her level of performance. More study is required; however, there appears to be a direct link between the female gender and the desire to exceed in a world dominated by men." Cheryl glared at David, unable to believe he had just said that, despite multiple conversations they had had on the subject.

Michael looked thoughtful. "That's well and good, and quite true, but I think we need to see what happens when a subject is asked to do more than just obtain some information or stand there and be scrutinised through examination. In regards to the need for the female to excel, well, personally I think that's a given."

Cheryl decided to ignore Michael's male chauvinism, but he did have a valid point in regard to upping the ante with the study. "We have already initiated that," stated Cheryl. "You see, Michael, Subject 003 is currently studying Subject 008, Thomas Christian."

"Oh yes - the former SOGGIE who fucked up, right?"

"Yep, that's the one. Well, we thought he was a bit ate-up, especially given what the former subjects had reported back to us about him, and also what he openly speaks to us about at The Agency. Well, a few weeks ago we gave his job file to Bianca and you wouldn't fucking believe it, but he actually told Bianca he worked for The Agency!"

Michael's eyes widened. "Holy shit, why wasn't I informed of this earlier?"

"Because we only just found out, Michael."

"Tell me, what did Bianca do?"

"We aren't one hundred percent sure yet. She's been called into the Agency tomorrow. We couldn't see her today, given that we needed to be here. She did text me, asking why she was studying one of our own."

Michael looked furious. "And you have full faith that she wouldn't have said anything back to him about herself? Fuck me, if she did, the whole project would be exposed!"

"After three years of studying this woman, I can tell you that she would have kept her mouth shut. She will be looking for answers though, that's a given."

"What are you going to tell her?" he asked, still sounding mad.

"Well, we'll just play on her ego like we normally do. Tell her that we had our suspicions about Thomas's ability to keep his mouth shut about the job. She'll be thrilled she was the one to uncover his weakness."

Michael seemed to calm down and he looked at the pair, hoping they were right.

"I certainly hope so. This does, however, make the study much more interesting now."

"Certainly does," agreed Cheryl. "Michael, as you mentioned, we need to up the ante with the study. Given the current situation, I would like to ask permission for The Agency to terminate subject 008? "

"Terminate?" Michael repeated. He had a serious look on his face. "Well, this will have to go further than me, but yes, I will make the recommendation given the situation. We can't have someone blurting about the Agency just walking around the joint. I will need a full written report by 1500 hours today to present to the Minister."

Cheryl smiled and looked at David. David looked pleased. "Absolutely, we will get it to you ASAP."

Michael picked up his coffee cup and walked out of the room. Suddenly he turned around and spoke. "Oh, by the way, who at The Agency will be undertaking the termination if it's approved?"

"Subject 003 of course."

CHAPTER 13

South Melbourne, Victoria

"FUCK ME DEAD CHERYL, what is going on?"

Cheryl smiled at her subject. "Well Bianca, you know there's a few people around here who wouldn't mind that, but right now is not the time."

Bianca wasn't impressed by her boss's attempt at humour. She had asked a serious question that required an immediate answer.

Cheryl continued, "Thomas Christian is exactly like you, Bianca. He is employed in the same role as you. Even though you haven't met them, there are plenty of other employees engaged to fulfil the same tasks as you. You are not the only one, you know."

"Yes I know that!" Bianca spluttered out. "Of course I know there are others, but why is a fellow employee my subject?"

"Oh Bianca, we really had more faith in you. We thought you would have worked that one out by now. Sometimes I really do question my confidence in you." Cheryl looked disappointed, but continued. "Thomas Christian is a complete live wire. He was recruited by The Agency when he left VICPOL, but recently we have been unsure of his ability to remain covert. I mean, confidentiality is everything. As you know, our clients pay big money and they have complete trust in our abilities. We can't have someone like him compromising us."

"So you got me in to see what he would tell me?" Bianca asked, still trying to analyse the information she had received.

"Of course. You are the best, Bianca, the best!" said Cheryl, suddenly contradicting herself from moments before. "And of course I made the right decision, because look at what has now unfolded. He fucking told you everything. We were right to have our suspicions and you were the right person for the job. Well done!"

"Well," Bianca blushed, "I'm not too sure what to say; thank you I guess. However, I was just doing my job..."

"And you've done a great job. However, in saying that there's a lot more work to be done." Cheryl raised her stainless steel water bottle to her mouth. Bianca remembered how Cheryl had told her not to drink from plastic water bottles, as they would give her cancer. She then recalled how the media had pushed that pretty much everything gives you cancer, apparently even a hickey.

Bianca cast her eye over her boss curiously. "What more can I do now? I got what you wanted out of him, didn't I?"

"Yes you did; but as I said before, he cannot be trusted."

"So fire him."

"It doesn't exactly work like that," David suddenly butted in.

Bianca looked at him thinking how unattractive the man was. He and Cheryl were such opposites of each other, yet they did seem to work well together. Well, at least The Agency had always appeared to Bianca to run smoothly, fluid and dynamic yet most certainly not transparent.

"We cannot have an employee walking around telling people about The Agency. What happens if he now feels more comfortable? It's easier to talk about things after you've told someone about it. The next thing you know he'll be telling his wife and God forbid, his old VICPOL mates. Can you imagine? It would destroy the business. We get clients because they trust us, which means they trust our employees. It all goes hand in hand." David moved his gaze to Cheryl. Cheryl took over. "We have never asked an agency employee to do this before, but I am asking you now. I would like you to terminate Thomas Christian. I know you are capable, Bianca. I have full faith in your abilities."

Bianca looked like a stunned mullet. She didn't know what to feel or say. She felt as if she was in some form of shock. Finally she came out of it and spoke. "There is no way I'm killing him. That's not my job. I didn't sign up for that."

"I'm actually surprised to hear you say that," Cheryl said in her most 'I'm so disappointed in you' voice. "I know you are not a mercenary by any means, but I really thought I could rely on you. The Agency is certainly in a predicament."

"It's not my mess to clean up," Bianca stated sternly.

"Don't worry. There won't be any mess, we'll sort out that side of things. You're close to him now. You are the best person to undertake this job with the least fuss. It sounds to me like you're going soft. Do you actually have some feelings for him?"

Bianca looked away, trying to hide what was evidently showing on her face.

"The man is a dick, Bianca. He'll never leave his wife and kids. One of these days he'll get caught out by his wife with his pants down around his ankles and then he'll be dead anyway - or at least ball-less. You'll be doing her a favour. Don't worry about the clean-up. We'll sort all that out. You just let me know when the job has been completed."

Bianca retorted defiantly, "Did you not hear me? I'm not doing it. As much of an arse-wipe as he is, I won't be the one who inflicts his just desserts. Surely there are others much more qualified to undertake this."

Cheryl looked mad and David inquisitive, but he remained silent as if he was watching Bianca's every reaction. It was actually the first time Bianca had noticed how intently he watched her. Before, she had assumed he had just been perving on her, but the man genuinely looked fascinated, if not a little worried.

"Your insubordination will not be tolerated. We may not be able to make you do this, but I am your boss and I can stand you down whenever I like. I am *so* disappointed in you, Bianca. You have been *such* a good employee, but when The Agency needs you the most, you can't come through."

David finally spoke, repeating Cheryl's words. "Yes, *so* disappointing." He walked out of the room shaking his head.

"I'm sorry," said Bianca, sounding emotional for the first

time in many years. "What's going to happen with Thomas?"

"I'm not sure yet. He is a real threat to us."

"Please don't get someone else to do it. He only told me because of the way I am!" Bianca cried, unintentionally reaffirming to Cheryl how good she was at her job.

"Oh Bianca, you really are such a F.I.G.J.A.M. aren't you?"

Bianca wasn't too sure what to make of that comment. Sure she knew what it meant, but Cheryl had said it almost affectionately.

Her boss continued, "In the meantime I don't want you to have anything to do with the man. If he texts you, ignore him. If he calls you, ignore him. And if he turns up at your place, fucking don't let him in. You know how to lie, you're an expert at it for God's sake!"

Bianca looked shattered and Cheryl could see it written all over her. "You can wait to hear from me for your re-assignment - that is, unless you change your mind, then you can contact me. Bianca, you are *very* lucky I'm so fond of you, otherwise you would probably now be unemployed."

David had watched as Bianca walked out of The Agency. She had honestly looked upset. This new display of emotion was concerning to the scientist. He walked into Cheryl's office where he found her already tapping away with her eyes on the screen. She glanced up at David.

"Well, that didn't quite go to plan, did it?" David asked with prominent worry lines.

Cheryl noticed the lines and thought he really could do with some of her favourite injectable. "Quite the contrary," stated Cheryl smiling. "I actually think she took it pretty well."

"But the fact that she hasn't agreed with our request throws a big spanner in the works. All those years of study suggested that she would be agreeable. I mean, she always does what we want ... well, maybe apart from the nose job, but that was only because of her phobia of being under." David paused for a moment, gathering his thoughts. "I'm fearful of how much she may actually like the guy."

"No, you are just fearful of the fact that you guessed wrong this time. You thought she would definitely just do it." David looked embarrassed and shuffled his feet on the floor.

Cheryl started tapping away again on her keyboard while continuing the conversation. "Well you don't have to be fearful, because I have full faith in our subject."

"I don't know, Cheryl. You saw her body language, she was extremely uncomfortable with the whole idea of Thomas being terminated. She has a real thing for him."

"Don't be stupid, David!" Cheryl snapped back. "You're having one of your stupid moments again. She knows the guy is as loose as they come, she called him an arse-wipe herself. She may momentarily find herself being caught in those blue eyes of his, but she won't catch herself in his trap."

"Yeah, I heard her say that, but that was also after you called him a dick. I might be out of place, but you are sounding jealous of the fact she may have feelings for him." David hoped that comment wouldn't find him out the office door, or through the office wall for that matter. He knew he was no match for Cheryl, despite their opposite genders.

"Jealous ha!" rebutted Cheryl. "I know where Bianca's loyalties lie. Now, stop that frowning, you're giving yourself more wrinkles!"

CHAPTER 14

Inner Eastern Suburbs, Melbourne, Victoria

"YOU NOT WORKING TODAY? You've been working heaps lately."

Thomas leant in and kissed his wife. "Well it's what I do, honey, to keep you in diamonds."

His wife laughed a little. *Well,* she thought, *I may not be dripping in diamonds but I do have a big collection of Tiffany Silver, Pandora and a one-and-a-half carat solitaire diamond sitting on my left ring finger.* She momentarily admired her ring, allowing herself to be caught up in its shimmering facets.

She came out of the ring's dazzling rapture. "The kids are in the living room, I think."

Thomas walked into the living room. His eight-year-old daughter Alda was sitting on the couch watching YouTube on her iPad. Thomas hoped it was just funny goats and nothing else. Xavier, who was four, was in front of the TV. They didn't even look up when Thomas entered the room.

"Hey kids."

No answer.

"Hey, Alda, Xavier, I'm home."

The children looked at their father. "Oh hi, Dad," said Alda, then immediately returned her attention to the iPad.

"Hi Daddy. Guess what?" asked the younger one.

"What's that?"

"I'm watching Power Rangers."

"Good for you then," Thomas replied, and walked out of the room. *Fucking Power Rangers*, he thought. *Would they never end?* That show was on when he was a teenager.

He suddenly heard the kids yelling. They were at it again. He thought someone must have changed the channel.

"Change it back!" he heard one cry.

"Make me!" said the other.

He couldn't even be bothered to try to sort it out. He thought how much easier conflict resolution had been in the police force. He did love his children, but sometimes he wished some of those tactics could be used on them. He had been very efficient at neutralising offenders. For a second he visualised having one of his children in a restraint that slowly tightened the more they gave attitude to him. He stood there caught up in the fantasy, but then he snapped out of it. He knew that the courts probably wouldn't see that behaviour as lawful chastisement, which would have been his defence to assault.

I haven't even been home for ten minutes and I need a drink already, he thought to himself.

He proceeded to the fridge and took a look inside. It was jammed packed and Thomas wondered how much had actually been spent on groceries that week. There was cheese and an assortment of deli meats, jams and condiments, packets of prepacked salad, Chinese takeaway from the other night, fruit juices, tubs of yogurt and so much milk it looked like he had shares in a dairy farm. He couldn't see any beer or bottles of wine. He checked the pantry cupboard and the wine rack. Nothing.

"Don't we have some alcohol in this house?"

"Alcohol?" asked his wife, "Why do you need a drink?"

Thomas's heart sank. He did love his wife, but after all these years she really didn't know him at all. He hoped she hadn't suddenly decided to convert the family to some strain of Islam, or even worse, turn him into a SNAG.

"Because I feel like one, Jody, that's all. I thought I asked you to pick some up when you were doing the groceries."

"Oh sorry," said his wife, not sounding sorry at all. "Just have a drink of water."

"I don't want just water," he snapped back. Thomas was annoyed. "What are we having for dinner anyway?"

"I'm going to make lasagne."

Thomas immediately thought of Bianca. She had said she wasn't a great cook, but her lasagne had been pretty damn good apart from a tiny bit of darkness where it had caught on the edges before she saved it. He knew his wife's wouldn't taste as nice.

He felt his phone vibrate. He left his wife inside and the kids who were still fighting, and sat out on his back deck, drink-less. Thomas looked at his mobile phone. It was Bianca.

After a few minutes Thomas came back inside and into the kitchen.

"Sorry, honey, but that was work. They need me to work again tonight."

His wife seemed to not mind; she seemed more interested in the quiz show on the television. Thomas had to give it to her, she did have a pretty good head on her shoulders. She always displayed an impressive level of general knowledge; she was just the type of person you wanted on your table at a trivia night.

"Piccadilly Circus!" she called out at the TV at the same time as a contestant buzzed their buzzer.

"Piccadilly Circus," the game show contestant stated.

"Piccadilly Circus is correct," the host commented.

Jody looked pleased with herself. Thomas could still hear the kids fighting. It now appeared to be over what side of the lounge they were sitting on.

Thomas made his way down the hall and to the main bathroom to have a shower. *A circus, yep, that's about right,* he couldn't help but think to himself.

CHAPTER 15

Outer Eastern Suburbs, Melbourne, Victoria

B IANCA RETURNED TO HER apartment to find Samson sunning himself on the floor where the afternoon sun had made its way through the blinds. He was a magnificent looking creature and Bianca understood why the ancient Egyptians had worshipped the animal.

She picked him up and gave him a cuddle. For a moment she thought about how he was her only real friend in the entire world. After a lengthy embrace, she put him back on the ground and went into the kitchen and grabbed a wineglass. She opened the fridge and pulled out a bottle of Lindeman's and started pouring. She looked down into the glass and spoke: "Actually, you are my friend too, and you always make everything better." The wine didn't reply.

Bianca walked into her living room and took a seat on her couch, relaxing back into it. Samson jumped up and joined her.

Her mind was a blur and she was having trouble computing what had just gone down at The Agency. She knew she needed to regain her composure and sort out her shit. She texted Thomas: *I need you here now.*

She received a text back: *Hey sexy, sorry but with the fam.*

Spending time with his family, Bianca thought. She then felt a strange feeling come over her. She had rarely experienced it before and it was making her blood boil. It was jealousy.

She sat there resembling a green-eyed monster for a moment before she received another text back from Thomas. *I can be there by 8.30pm X,* the text read. She suddenly felt better because she now felt wanted, and it was reassurance that she wasn't a loser who couldn't do her job. She took a couple of big swigs of wine and headed for the bathroom, thinking she'd better shower and get herself looking good for Thomas. She might even try to clean her fingernails ...

"I hope you already ate, because I haven't made dinner for us," Bianca asserted as she opened her front door for her subject.

"It's okay, I already ate. Jody made me lasagne."

Bianca coughed. It was the first time she had heard Thomas say his wife's name. Even though he had never actually said it before, she knew it was her. She felt that feeling re-entering her body.

Thomas must have sensed the change in Bianca and quickly continued, "And your lasagne is heaps better." He gave her a kiss on the cheek. His lips were soft and his beard felt reassuring on her face. She immediately felt the monster inside lurking away again.

She noticed he hadn't brought any wine with him on this visit. Bianca thought it lucky that she kept a stockpile that would rival Bottlemart.

"You want a wine?" she asked him.

"Yeah of course, I mean that's if you're having one."

"Of course I'm having one."

"Yes of course you are, you're an alcoholic," Thomas laughed. Bianca wasn't so sure about the joke on her. Yes, she had joked to him about being an alcoholic that one time, but she didn't think that gave him permission to call her one. She decided to ignore the comment and just get the man a drink.

"So how is everything going? Your book, the spying, your *family*...?"

Thomas surveyed her. She had asked that with a tone in her voice that he couldn't quite put his finger on. Overall, her disposition seemed a bit different. Thomas thought she still looked hot as hell, maybe even more attractive, as if she had made an extra effort tonight yet somehow still maintained a casual appearance. But despite her looks, she just seemed a bit "off".

"Well the book is coming on slowly; I haven't really written much since I last saw you."

Bianca interrupted him, "Oh, I thought I might be that muse you have been looking for." She lowered her head and looked into her glass. The wine just stared blankly back at her like Salar de Uyuni.

"I haven't written much because I've been too busy think-ing about you." Thomas smiled and put his hand on her leg, "You're too much of a distraction, girl." He leaned in and kissed her.

As her tongue met his, Bianca thought what an awesome kisser he was. She climbed back into her favourite position, straddling him and locking him in as if she was about to compete in a rodeo.

Bianca pulled away from Thomas's mouth and looked into his perfect cornflower eyes. It was time for the moment of truth. "If I said to you that I have an appointment scheduled, what would you think?"

"I dunno, I would think maybe you were getting your hair done. You certainly don't need to get your bikini line waxed." Thomas laughed at his own joke, thinking about Bianca's bare bits. Bianca wasn't laughing. The look on her face was dead serious, the most serious he had seen on her. Thomas stopped laughing and his jaw dropped. Bianca was still straddling him with a tight grip and for a moment he felt compromised.

"You're got to be fucking kidding me, right. There's no way."

She stayed in position, "Yes way."

Thomas violently rose up from his seat, causing Bianca to fall onto the other side of the couch and almost off it. She noted what a lightweight she was compared to him.

Thomas found himself pacing across the living room. Samson was now wide awake on the armchair watching Thom-as's every move. A Crowded House song was playing from the iPod. He couldn't make out which one it was, as apart from the fact that his head was spinning, they all sounded the same to him.

"Why didn't you tell me?" he finally asked.

"Because as you know we are not supposed to tell ... *anyone*."

Thomas heard the disdain in her voice, alerting him to the fact that she had obviously been disappointed in him when he had revealed his position to her. He then thought, *Who does she think she is? She's just told me, she's no better than me.*

"Well, that's a bit of the pot calling the kettle black." Thomas continued, looking her slim frame up and down. "I can't believe you work for The Agency too." He was shaking his head in disbelief.

Bianca didn't like the way he had said that. It felt to her that she appeared to him as though she would be incapable of doing the job.

"Why don't you get off your fucking high horse and get yourself back on the ground. You walk around like your shit doesn't stink. I can tell you, though, I know that your shit does stink. You are also a walking contradiction of yourself. You can't be trusted, that's why The Agency got me to study you."

"They got you to study me?" Thomas asked, looking shocked.

"What - you think we just randomly met? My God, you're amazing!" said Bianca, laughing at his ignorance.

He sat back down on the couch and lowered his head. He was fuming, but he knew he was angrier at himself than anything else. Angry at himself for not picking her out, and more angry for revealing himself to her. *Thomas*, he thought to himself, *you are a bloody idiot.*

"I'm going to get us some more wine," Bianca said, getting off the couch that she was only half on and made her way into the kitchen. Her tone had changed and it was almost as if the conversation hadn't even happened.

Thomas was still seated on the couch trying to unravel his own ball of confusion when Bianca reappeared with two wine fishbowls. She put them down on the coffee table and took a seat right in next to him.

"So why have *you* decided to tell *me*?" he finally asked. "You know we aren't supposed to tell anyone, as you have already so blatantly pointed out to me."

Bianca moved in even closer so one of her breasts was up against his chest. She spoke softly and touched his face at the same time. "Because I may be in love with you."

"Oh." Thomas looked at her and realised how absolutely stunning he found her. He had really liked her before, but now knowing that she also worked for The Agency, well this changed everything. He may have been angry, but he quickly realised that the anger should be directed at himself, not at her. *She was only doing her job*, he thought. *And she has done a pretty good job.* He found himself suddenly very impressed by the woman, though maybe even a little envious.

"Obviously, this is a complete shock for me, the whole Agency thing. I can't believe they didn't trust me!" Thomas took a big drink of his wine. God only knows he needed it. He continued, "I have to say, though, that for someone whom I've only known for a short time, I am very taken with you. I don't think I've ever fallen for someone as quickly as I did with you. It was as if you shot me straight through the chest."

Bianca smiled and climbed back onto his lap. She brushed her hand down his face and across his spiky chin. "Glad to hear that." She smiled a sweet smile and kissed him softly on the lips.

"Hey, do you know what type of reprisal I will get once they find out I told you first?"

"Who's saying they will find out? I'm the only one that knows, remember?" Bianca gave him another kiss and continued. "You better have some more wine. After what's just happened, I think we need to bang the angry out of each other."

CHAPTER 16

Outer Eastern Suburbs, Melbourne, Victoria

B IANCA WAS LOOKING AT her body in the bathroom mirror. She had quite a number of bruises. Unfortunately, she had always bruised easily and after last night's activities this now meant that her skin displayed shades of blue, purple and green.

Hmm, what to tell Cheryl at the next wellness check? Bianca thought. Hopefully they would be gone by then, but bruises seemed to hang around on her like a bad smell. She couldn't tell her the truth. Cheryl would be mad and Bianca was already not in her good books. Bianca had quickly learnt that she was one woman you did not get on the wrong side of, which was why Bianca had always tried to stay on the women's right side. She concluded that maybe she would just tell her boss that she picked up some hottie at her local bar. A tradie that was out looking for a good time. Bianca hadn't practised that type of behaviour outside of the job since she was twenty-five, but she knew she still had the goods to do it.

Bianca stepped into the shower and the warm water felt good on her battered body. It had been one hell of a rough night. Banging the angry out of each other had been an understatement. She hadn't been prepared for how rough Thomas would be with her. The man had really seemed set on putting on a large display of strength and showing her his virility.

One moment he had called her his little Agency slut and the next she was back to being *Biancaneve*. It excited Bianca and made her back up against him harder. She knew he was enjoying himself too. Although his anger with the whole Agency situation had been evident, he seemed to have come to some inner resolution and appeared pleased that together they would share their little secret.

Fuck, she suddenly thought. *I've told him I hadn't - and wouldn't - tell The Agency. What happens if next time he goes in there, they actually say something to him?* He would then know that she had lied, and the last thing Bianca wanted was for him not to trust her. Trust was everything in a relationship.

She once again swore at herself for the oversight. "Rookie mistake," she said to herself shaking her wet hair. Her mind settled as she realised that The Agency wouldn't be saying anything to him about her. They needed everything to be as normal as possible, because if preparations were being put in place, they would need him to be none the wiser.

Bianca lathered up her long legs with her scented body wash. She wished Thomas was still there to rub the soapy substance all over her, but he had left early, saying that as much as he wanted to stay with her, he had to get home.

She pictured what he would do before walking in the door. He would have to have some sort of grab bag in the back of his car for sure. He would almost definitely stop at some large service station with extensive facilities including showers for the truckies. She visualised him pulling the bag out of the boot of his Range Rover and taking it into the showers. He would have a shit and a shower, but no shave since it appeared he was trying to grow his beard. He'd put on his security job clothes and then drive home hoping that Jody and the kids were already on the road for the school drop-off.

Well he's an idiot if he doesn't do that, because he's covered in me. If I was him, that's what I would do for sure, thought Bianca.

She finished showering and washing her brunette hair. She stepped out of the shower, grabbed her Sheridan towel and proceeded to only half-dry herself while looking at herself randomly in the bathroom mirror at various angles. All those years of ballet and basketball had really paid off. She truly believed she was in the best shape of her life. At least six kilos lighter than she was when she was eighteen years old. Bianca opened her panties drawer, grabbed a pair of Bonds cotton knickers and put them on. Maybe not the sexiest of lingerie choices in many people's opinion, but they were undoubtedly practical. She also took out her weapon case, and placed the grey box on the bed. She threw her designer t-shirt on, not bothering with a bra. Samson had entered the room and was curling around her ankles. He started to meow.

"I know, baby, Mummy will get you some food in a minute, okay?"

Bianca knelt down next to her bed and recovered her Beretta 92 pistol from its hiding place. She checked the safety, pressed the magazine release button and caught the mag in her hand. She then racked the slide with the weapon on a slight angle until the bullet that was sitting in the chamber came out. Bianca safety checked the pistol again and placed it into its special grey bed along with the magazine.

"Come on, boy, Mummy will get you your yummies now."

Somewhere in North East Victoria

Bring bring, bring bring, Margaret could hear her husband's phone ringing.

"Tony, that's your mobile, someone's trying to call you."

"I know, I know, I can hear it." Tony made it just in time and answered the phone. He hadn't even had a chance to look at the phone number.

"Hello." There was silence. "Oh, Bianca! *Ciao, cara!*"

"Is that Bianca? Tell her I said hello, okay?" Margaret called out to Tony from the farmhouse kitchen where she was sorting out the eggs that had been collected that morning.

"Margaret says hello. How have you been? Long time, no hear."

After about twenty minutes on the phone, Tony made his

way back into the kitchen where his wife had started chopping up their home-grown vegetables for the slow cooked casserole that would be their dinner that night.

"That was Bianca, ha? She hasn't phoned in ages. How is she? What did she want?"

"She wants to come for a visit … *soon*."

Margaret was thrilled to hear the news. A big smile spread across her face. She had always liked Bianca, despite the fact she chose to live in the city and didn't have much to do with her own family. It was evident to Margaret and Tony that Bianca liked them too, because despite everything she had managed to maintain some form of contact with them.

"That's great news. When is she due?" Margaret asked, planning to check the bed in the spare room and put out her Crabtree and Evelyn guest soaps. She wanted to make sure everything was perfect for her favourite niece.

"Not exactly sure yet, but soon. She said she'd let me know within the next couple of days. Oh, and she's going to bring her cat."

"That's okay, I don't mind Samson, I just won't let him out near the chooks," replied Margaret thinking about her ribbon-winning silky.

"That's not all she's bringing. She's bringing a man."

Margaret's eyes lit up like a fireworks display.

"A man? Wow, how exciting. I'm *so* glad to hear that. How long have they been together? What's his name?"

"I don't know, Margaret, I didn't ask those questions. I'm not a woman, you know."

Tony was glad he wasn't a woman. He liked his grappa, his hunting and his wife's large breasts way too much to be a woman.

"Well, I'm just glad she has finally found herself a man. You know we all had our concerns about her." Margaret gave her husband a look that said *you know what I'm talking about.*

Tony ignored the look. Despite his strong Catholic upbringing, he wasn't as uptight as his wife about certain things. Tony made his way out of the kitchen. The slasher was beckoning him to come do some work.

"Did she say why she wanted to visit now?" Margaret asked, moving onto slicing potatoes.

"Yeah, she needs to borrow something from me."

CHAPTER 17

South Melbourne, Victoria

"**I** KNOW THAT YOU got Bianca Beretta to study me."

Cheryl and David just looked at each other.

Thomas continued, "Yeah she told me. The woman is in love with me."

Cheryl thought about how the man really didn't think through what he said before he spoke. He could have played this so many other ways, but instead he was just going to make out that Bianca had revealed herself to him. What a dick move. She looked at David, indicating wordlessly: *I'll let you have this one.*

"Christo, mate. Of course we got Bianca to study you. I'm a guy, so I feel a bit strange saying this, but you are by far the best-looking of all our employees." He paused. "Well, maybe except Bianca, but as you now know, she's pretty damn gorgeous."

Thomas still looked pissed off, as if he might flatten David any second. David continued, "As I was saying, we got her to study you because we knew she would fall for you. I mean come on, we know about your long and distinguished list - you just have to smile and it makes the women pool."

David thought about what he had said and he was jealous of the ability that Thomas had. It was like some superhuman power. He would have given away at least fifty percent of his brain capacity for that type of ability.

"But why did you want her to fall for *me*?" Thomas asked.

"Come on Christo, you should be able to work that one out. It was so she would reveal herself to you. You see, she can't be trusted, she is our only female employee in the role and we were concerned that once she fell for someone every-thing would come blurting out. And of course it did, just as we suspected." David started to take a little walk around the room. Thomas was still standing up with his broad back blocking the doorway.

"She said that you guys got her to study me for basically the same reason, that you didn't trust me?"

Cheryl decided she'd better take over. She didn't want David to stuff it up; she was much better than him at this sort of thing. "Of course that's what she said. That's what we told her!" She noticed that Thomas was starting to look as if he was questioning what was going on. Cheryl knew better than to let her subjects think too much.

"As David said, we took on Bianca here at the Agency because I thought she had potential. Being a woman myself I also thought it was only fair that we give a woman a go at the position. Bianca seemed to be a good candidate. Unfortunately I was wrong. Women don't belong in certain positions. They are too soft and they let their emotions get in the way."

Thomas sat down. His head was a mess, but he felt better about himself. *So The Agency did trust him*, he concluded. They were never concerned about him, they were only concerned about their female employee revealing more than her breasts. He felt good, although a touch guilty. It was he who had revealed himself to Bianca first, but they didn't need to know that. *Just like my wife*, he thought, *what they don't know won't hurt them*.

Cheryl continued with her rant, "Unfortunately though, Thomas, we now have a problem. Bianca is fucking in love with you and she has revealed her position at the Agency. She can't be trusted at all. She knows all about your wife and family, doesn't she?"

Thomas nodded his head.

"Well you, Thomas, now also have a big problem. Once you decide you've had enough of her sugar she'll be pissed and she will tell your wife about the affair. Put money on it. Your wife will take you to the cleaners. You won't see your kids, she'll get the house and probably that Range Rover of yours too. Yep, you'll be cleaned out." Cheryl grabbed her water bottle and drank from it right on cue.

"You really think she will tell?" Thomas asked with alarm in his voice.

"Come on, the woman is insane. We have seen sides of her that would make you shudder."

Thomas did suddenly shudder, thinking back to Bianca's comment about psycho women actually acting rationally. He then remembered her brown eyes. They were trusting eyes, not crazy bitch ones.

"Bianca has now compromised the integrity of the business. As you are well aware, when every employee signs up, they agree to the strictest of confidentiality agreements. Bianca has broken that agreement. We cannot have her with us anymore." Cheryl came in closer to Thomas. Her Veronika Maine blouse-covered breasts were near his face.

"Your current subject, Gary Stephenson, has been reassigned. You now have a new job." Cheryl glanced over at David and then back to Thomas. "We want you to terminate Bianca."

What? Had he heard right? He asked himself. He had told them about Bianca thinking they would just dismiss her, not this though. *Fuck*, he thought, *lucky I got in first!*

Cheryl saw the look on his face and so continued, "By doing this, it will solve all your problems and of course clean up the mess for The Agency as well. Doing it will prove your loyalty to us. You already stuffed up one career. You don't want to stuff up this one do you, not to mention your marriage?"

Thomas just sat there with a look of bewilderment on his face. Eventually he spoke, "I don't think I can do that."

Cheryl glared at him. "Actually, you have no choice."

"We haven't had authorisation for that," David stated looking concerned.

"Don't worry, he won't do it. He's too much of a pussy." A grin spread across Cheryl's face. "Actually, what I should say is that he's too pussy-whipped. You wait and see, he'll come back in here with some lame excuse as to why he couldn't get rid of her."

"What happens if we're wrong, and he does do it?"

"Well that will make for some very interesting findings then, won't it?" Cheryl took a swig from her water bottle and continued, "As much as we all like having Bianca around, she has been studied for a number of years now and yes she has presented some interesting findings, but hey if 008 terminates her, it will be the most interesting of all."

David smiled, his boss was right. Imagine the data he could collate and present to the Department if that played out? He smiled inside a little bit more. It would definitely save The Agency, and if Canberra wasn't so tight arsed then a big promotion could be coming his way. God knows he was due for one. His smiled dropped as he suddenly had a thought.

"Cheryl, what's the plan if Thomas and Bianca don't take each other out? I mean, we haven't heard anything from her yet."

"Oh David, you should know me well enough by now to know I already have a contingency plan."

David looked at his boss with a grin. *That woman always has a plan,* he thought.

She is clothed with strength and dignity and she laughs without fear of the future

Prov. 31:25

Outer Eastern Suburbs, Melbourne, Victoria

B IANCA ENDED THE CALL on her Samsung. She smiled to herself. She could always rely on her uncle.

She realised she actually had a bit of time to herself - well, apart from her cat being there. Samson wasn't any annoyance or interruption, though. She loved him. If anyone ever tried to hurt him she would have to put cold steel into their femoral artery.

Bianca walked into the kitchen and opened up the fridge. Unfortunately, its contents were starting to dissipate and she cringed at the thought of having to negotiate the local supermarket once again. She found some cheese and decided that would do for the time being to get her through until dinner. She leant down and gave Samson a little piece. He loved cheese, especially the stinky stuff, just like his owner. Her phone started ringing.

"Thomas? You calling me?"

"Yeah, I wanted to hear your voice."

"Of course you did."

The pair laughed over the line.

"I need to come over. I mean, I need to come over today."

"I'm home," Bianca replied.

The line went dead. Bianca checked her phone. Yep - he had definitely just ended the call.

Well, that was a bit rude, she thought. She also found it a turn-on at the same time. It was lucky that she hadn't made any other plans for the evening. She was just dressed in her Celine Paris t-shirt and Bonds panties. Bianca still hadn't bothered to put proper pants on. She remembered what one guy she had dated had once said to her, "I prefer you without pants." She also preferred herself without pants.

Bianca opened her front door to find Thomas with a super sexy look in his eye. Before she even had a chance to say hello, he shut the door behind himself and grabbed her, pulling her into him. Bianca couldn't help but be automatically aroused and she relaxed, letting her tongue find his. He threw off his coat and then lifted Bianca up with her long legs wrapping around his waist. Bianca was impressed by this show of strength and wondered how long he could endure it. She was extremely happy to find out he could hold her in that position for long enough to make profanities come out of her mouth and other sounds out of his.

Once they were done, she pulled back her panties and tousled her hair back into place. "Hello Thomas."

"Well hello," was the reply.

Thomas noticed Samson just sitting there near the doorway staring at him. He had a look of utter disgust on his face. *Yes, that's right Samson, I just fucked your mother. How'd you like them apples?* He wished like hell he could actually verbalise it to the over-possessive cat.

"Come into the living room, give yourself a moment of R and R," Bianca said as she made her way from the apartment entrance.

"You are my R and R," Thomas responded.

Bianca blushed. *Sometimes the man could be sweet as sugar,* she thought. She then remembered her hatred for the white substance.

Thomas took a seat on the couch. Bianca had noticed that if the left side was free, he always chose that same side to sit on. She couldn't help but think how predictable he was, not a great trait for people in their field of employment.

Bianca took the seat next to him. Samson decided to take the armchair. The cat was obviously still coming to terms with its retina burn. Bianca noted it was strange behaviour for a cat that usually didn't give a flying fuck.

"I'm going to the country for a day or two and I want you to join me," Bianca stated casually.

Thomas pondered on her surprise request before speaking. "Why do you want me to come with you?"

"Look, it's just something I need to do to get my family off my back. You would be doing me a *big* favour, that's all." Bianca suddenly realised she hadn't been the hostess with the mostest and offered him a drink. She then decided they'd better finish this conversation before it was somehow diverted off on another tangent.

"I'd like to help you out, but I mean..." Thomas paused, "I just can't."

Bianca looked at Thomas. He looked phlegmatic, kind of like herself she thought.

"What do you mean you *just can't*?" she asked, trying not to let any emotion show. "You should be an expert liar, you should be able to just make up some excuse to your family for needing to be away for a few days. I mean if you can't do that, then..."

Thomas knew what Bianca was getting at. She was questioning his prowess. He quickly dismissed it; he was well aware of his own capabilities. He was also aware of his priorities and responsibilities, and as much of a circus as it was at home, he understood where the line in the sand lay.

Thomas leaned in and put his hand through her hair. "Bianca, baby. I know you have really strong feelings for me and to be honest, I actually think I could be in love with you too."

Bianca's heart almost missed a beat hearing her subject say that. She'd never had anyone say it to her so quickly. *Cheryl had been right*, she thought, *he really was different.*

Thomas continued on: "However, in saying that, I just can't. I mean, I think you might want a proper relationship and I just can't, it would kill her."

Bianca knew he was referring to his wife. She smiled reluctantly and said, "It's okay, I understand."

Thomas kept gently stroking her hair. "I knew you would. It's better this way, don't you think? It's our secret." He gave her a little kiss on the mouth and continued, "I think about you all the time."

Bianca smiled at Thomas and ran her fingers across his chest. "Yeah, I guess it is better this way. Who'd wanna get into one of those rut relationships anyhow?" Bianca immediately got up and made her way into the kitchen. Thomas knew her well enough by now to know she would be fixing them a drink.

As predicted, she entered the living room holding two wine-glasses. Samson was still on the armchair eyeballing Thomas.

Bianca couldn't help but notice Thomas's face. "You have a look on your face that says you might be needing a drink. "

"Yes, well we both will be needing a drink. You'd better take a seat."

Bianca looked at him curiously. *What could he possibly say to her to make her need a drink more than she already did?*

"I didn't just come here to tell you I think about you all the time," Thomas stated.

"Yeah well, actually I thought you were just here to fuck my brains out."

Thomas smiled and answered, "Yes, well that too."

Bianca took a sip of her wine. "Well tell me, why else did you want to come around, then?"

She noticed the very serious look on Thomas's face, and wasn't sure what to make of it.

"Well, I was summoned to The Agency today and..." his voice faded off.

Oh crap, Bianca thought, *they've told him that I told them first, crap, crap.*

"They have asked me to kill you."

Once again, Bianca had to hold herself back from spitting wine all over the man, despite him being shirtless this time. "Excuse me?"

Thomas had an almost bemused look on his face.

"No, I think you have your wires crossed there, Thomas. Why would they ask you to kill *me*?"

Thomas took a drink of his wine and kept Bianca hanging for the answer longer than she felt was necessary given the context of the conversation.

"Because they believe that you can't be trusted, being a woman and all." He took another sip of wine and Bianca couldn't help but notice the complacency of his tone. It was lucky for him that Samson wasn't in her hands, because that comment made her want to throw the cat at his face and watch what happened.

Bianca sat silently, staring blankly ahead. Thomas moved in close to her and put his arm around her, squeezing her tightly. Thomas loved how little her waist was. He spoke to break the silence. "Don't worry, I would never lay a finger on you. Not a finger, baby." Bianca immediately flashed back to the other night where during their "angry" sex Thomas had hit her so hard it had actually brought a tear to her eye.

"You were right, I definitely needed the drink." Bianca poured a large amount of the contents of her glass down her throat. "What would make them think I can't be trusted? Especially after I've worked for them for so long?"

Thomas had a stupid look on his face which Bianca was immediately suspicious of. "I don't know, I'm just relaying what they said to me. They only tell you what you need to know and that's what they told me."

Bianca continued her questioning, "So they asked you today, when you were in there?"

"Yep, they asked me to do it. They have reassigned my current subject, Gary Stephenson."

Outer Eastern Suburbs, Melbourne, Victoria

BIANCA'S EAR PRICKED UP. Gary Stephenson. She knew that name. Actually, she knew that name *very* well.

"Did you just say Gary Stephenson?"

"Yeah, he's the subject I'd started studying, before The Agency had a change of plans for me..." Thomas looked away, realising this information might be hard for Bianca to take. Despite the Berlin-type wall she put up, he knew she was still human and not only that, a woman.

"The Columbian."

Thomas glared at her. *How did she know Gary hung out at The Columbian?*

Bianca may have been an expert linguist, but she also wasn't bad at interpreting body language. She could tell immediately that she had the right Gary Stephenson.

"Gary Stephenson was one of my first subjects, Thomas. This doesn't make sense at all," Bianca stated, shaking her head.

Thomas appeared to be deliberating on her comment. He finally spoke. "Well, maybe you didn't obtain all the information that was required. Maybe you missed something first time round."

Bianca shot him daggers. Thomas felt them pierce him. It was her retaliation for questioning her aptness. Thomas retorted, "Well, you did just say that he was one of your first subjects. It's okay to still be learning, then."

Bianca wouldn't submit to Thomas's train of thought. She knew herself better than that.

"I got everything out of him, Thomas. Absolutely everything."

He could tell by Bianca's tone that she was serious and that she really had got *everything* out of the man.

"So I'm guessing you fucked him?" he said in a jealous tone.

Bianca immediately retaliated. "Don't get narky with me now, you know we do what we need to do."

Thomas looked down at the apartment floorboards, then back at Bianca. He pictured Gary with Bianca sitting on his lap. He cringed. He didn't know how she could even kiss a smoker, let alone have sex with the guy. Subject or not, from what he had seen, Gary was a complete loser.

"I don't know, Bianca, the guy's a mess and he stinks; I don't know how you could..."

Bianca interrupted before he could finish his sentence. "Gary Stephenson is actually a very kind-hearted person, plus *he* wasn't married at the time, he was widowed actually."

"Yeah, I know that about him having lost his wife and daughter; that was in the job file. In terms of him being a nice person, well, I really didn't get a chance to see that side."

Bianca suddenly realised how pleased she was to hear that Gary was alive and kicking. *So nothing had happened to him after her studies,* she thought, and couldn't help but smile inside. This was welcome news to her. As much as she was usually non-emotional in regards to her subjects, she'd always had a soft spot for him despite his pitfalls and tormented mind.

She started running her fingers across Thomas's chest again. She couldn't deny it, he did have a great chest. It was muscular, but certainly not resembling Arnold Schwarzenegger in *Pumping Iron* which was actually a blessing. She felt inclined to touch it, especially after Thomas had exhibited such jealousy in front of her. Bianca thought it best to give the guy some reassurance.

Thomas liked the feel of her fingers on him. He thought how well Bianca was taking the news he had just told her. *The woman really is stolid. If I had just been told that, I would have gone postal by now.*

Although Thomas still found it slightly hard to believe her ability to service her former subject, he quickly realised that he would need to get over that. *She obviously only has eyes for me,* he thought, as Bianca calmly sat there brushing her fingers across his body and taking intermittent sips of her wine. He noted, however, that her gaze showed she was a million miles away.

"Bianca, are you okay?"

"As always I'm just fine. I was just thinking."

"Naturally," said Thomas. "I mean, given what I've just told you, you're going to need to think about your next move. I'm not going to kill you, I could never do that to you. Look, I'm sure I'll be reprimanded for it, but I don't give a flying fuck. If they fire me, I'll be able to pick up another job like that." Thomas clicked his fingers.

Bianca shook her head and said, "No Thomas, I wasn't thinking about that, I was thinking about Gary Stephenson being your subject."

"You need to drop that, Bianca. You have much bigger things to worry about!" Thomas couldn't believe the woman was so conceited she couldn't accept that she probably hadn't performed as well as she thought.

"Do you know which employee Gary has been reassigned to?" Bianca asked.

"No of course not. You know we employees don't know each other. Well, apart from you and me now. The Agency keeps us separated for a reason, to maintain the highest level in confidentiality."

"Yeah okay, I was just checking." Bianca took another sip of wine and continued, "Thomas, I think we need to make a visit to The Columbian."

Thomas laughed. "Come on, Bianca, that job's done and dusted. You really need to concentrate on not getting yourself killed now. If I was you, I'd make contact with Cheryl and arrange to get that hot arse of yours into The Agency to apologise and submit your resignation. In my opinion termination is very drastic, so if you beg for forgiveness and tell them you'll never speak a word, it might be enough to make them change their mind about you. As I said, I'm not going to do it, but they might get some other fucker onto it and I really don't want that for you." Thomas looked at her lovingly.

"No Thomas, the Gary thing isn't right. It's not sitting well with me at all." Bianca had that feeling in her gut.

"Really, Bianca? You really want to go see Gary?"

"No, not Gary per se, we need to study the Columbian to see who is now studying him."

"But why? What good is that going to do?"

Thomas had no idea what was going on inside the woman's head. He looked into her eyes and as if they were windows inside her head, he could see a million cogs churning away. He just couldn't work out what the cogs were ticking away so hard for.

Bianca stared back into Thomas's eyes. All of a sudden, she felt that the man was more brawn then brains. She had thought that originally both were equal, making him a fine specimen; but over the past couple of days, some of the things he had said and done caused her to question her faith in his intellect.

"Because we need to make sure we don't recognise that person too!" Bianca exclaimed.

Thomas shook his head, "Baby, you have completely lost me."

Bianca stopped touching his chest and got up off the couch. She started to pace around the living room. Thomas thought how sexy she was in just her panties and t-shirt. He wished his wife would walk around the house like that - it might make him want to have sex with her more.

Samson jumped off the armchair and stretched his back, arching it right up. He looked at Thomas, then left the two alone in the living room. Thomas guessed he had had enough of his owner's gibberish.

Bianca's work phone lit up. *Shit*, she thought. She'd left it lying on the lamp table. She was mad at herself for such a complacent mistake. Thomas saw it and grabbed it from the table.

"Hand it over and don't touch my phone again," snapped Bianca.

Thomas was taken aback by the fierceness in Bianca's voice. "Geez, it's all right, calm down babe." Thomas handed over the phone and Bianca quickly snatched it from him. She didn't open the message but instead powered the device off.

"That was Cheryl, you know? I saw her name flash up when I grabbed it. You'd better text her back, she's probably wanting you to come in."

"She can wait," Bianca said in a tone that Thomas didn't like. Bianca noticed the look on Thomas's face and felt bad for being so abrasive with him.

She took a seat back on the couch next to him. She leant in close and kissed his mouth gently. "I'm sorry, I didn't mean to snap at you, but I'm just a bit on edge now." She took another drink of wine, hoping that might take her back to her usual sterile self.

"It's okay, completely understandable given everything." Thomas resumed kissing her and he put his hands back up under her t-shirt, working the piece of clothing off her. He pulled her onto him, making her sit right on top of him, in what Thomas believed to be Bianca's favourite position for lovemaking.

Thomas pulled her panties aside and slide himself inside her. Bianca thought the guy really did have a rapacious appetite. She knew better than to speak too much during sex, but she did need to ask him one more question.

"So you'll come to The Columbian with me then, you know, just to put my mind at rest?"

"If that's what we need to do to stop you from worrying that pretty little head of yours, then I'll come."

Not long after that Thomas did come, but then quickly left. He knew he'd spent too many nights lately away from the family, and as ignorant as his wife was of his behaviour, she certainly wasn't stupid.

Bianca lay back on the couch, thinking about the day's events and the conversations she and Thomas had had. *Kill me? Yeah right*, she thought, smiling to herself. She obviously knew Cheryl *way* better than Thomas did. Her concern, though, was Gary Stephenson. That was so weird and it definitely needed further investigation. She just wanted to go to sleep there and then, but she needed to do something first. She got up and picked up her phone from the TV unit and powered it back on. She wrote a text to Cheryl and sent it off. Cheryl immediately replied: *'Your appointment is scheduled for Thursday at 1000hrs.'* Bianca lay back down on the couch and closed her eyes. She really was fucked.

CHAPTER 20

North Melbourne, Victoria

"WHERE ARE YOUR SUNGLASSES?" Bianca hissed at Thomas.

"Oh shit," Thomas said as he patted his face and the top of his head.

Fucking hopeless, Bianca thought, but she didn't voice it.

Thomas rummaged through his man bag and pulled out a pair of Ray Bans and put them on. Bianca liked him in the sunnies, they suited his face and made him especially good-looking.

"What have you done with your hair?"

"Don't worry, I haven't cut it all off, it's just tucked up under."

"Hmm, smart."

"Yeah. Gary has seen us both before so we don't want him recognising us now."

Bianca was wearing a bohemian style floppy hat with Christian Dior sunglasses. She had on a matching top and

BROOKE STRAHAN

culottes set. Once again the weather had returned to its usual behaviour, so a long coat adorned her. She resembled a style blogger.

Thomas was impressed by her efforts. He thought that he probably would have just walked straight by her amongst the hustle and bustle of the street.

They had met at a café. This one was different from the one Bianca had previously chosen to stalk out Thomas. The busy street had a number of cafés all within close proximity to The Columbian. They were lucky for Melbourne's out-of-control caffeine addiction.

"Now, you know I'm just doing this for you because you asked so sweetly the other day."

"Yeah I know, and I thank you. I would have just done it by myself, but I really needed you here to see if you recognise anyone going in or out of the pub."

Thomas shook his head. The whole thing still didn't make sense to him, but he needed to keep Bianca happy. He had said no to her when she asked him to go to the country with her, so he had thought he'd better do this. He remembered what they had said at the Agency about her going and telling his wife. He didn't believe she would do it, though, since Bianca clearly enjoyed the affair way too much to stuff it up.

The pair ordered coffees and then some lunch. Bianca noticed that Thomas was back on the sugar. She had seen him put the devil into both of the coffees he had gone through since their arrival. She decided to pull in her sugar Nazi head and let it slide.

• 142 •

It appeared to everyone else that the two were having some type of work-lunch meeting, mainly due to the fact that papers lay spread out all over the table. These of course had been pre-prepared, and both were in fact intently studying The Columbian and all who entered and left.

Bianca thought she'd been studying it harder, as Thomas seemed easily distracted by any attractive woman who walked past him. She even caught him checking out a girl that must have been only around fourteen years of age. *Fucking men,* she thought, *unbelievable.*

"Brad Saunders," Bianca suddenly said.

"Sorry, what was that?" Thomas asked turning his head back from where it had been following a pair of tight Levi's.

"Brad Saunders. That's fucking Brad Saunders. Yep, that's definitely him."

"Who's Brad Saunders?"

"The guy that just entered the pub, the one with the navy-blue jacket and blackish hair. Didn't you see him?"

Thomas looked sheepish. "Actually no, sorry, I was trying to see if I recognised anyone on the street."

"Well the guy that just entered through the main doors is Brad Saunders. One hundred percent." Bianca sounded excited but nervous as well. Thomas could tell she was speaking the truth.

"You don't know Brad Saunders?" she asked with anticipation.

"No, I don't. Never heard that name in my life."

"Well I do. He was one of my subjects."

This time it was Thomas's turn to almost spit out his beverage all over Bianca.

"Let me guess, you fucked him too."

Bianca paused and took a sip of her coffee. She was impressed at how long she had made that particular cup last. "That would be correct."

"Well I'm sure he was better than Gary." Thomas thought how much that man unimpressed him. He may at one point in time have been some type of Tony Stark wannabe, but now he was just a drunk.

"He was all right, just typical green slime," Bianca stated in a matter-of-fact manner.

"What, he was a slimy prick?"

"No. Well, kinda. You know green slime? Army IntellO?" Bianca continued, "Well anyway, he has real bad PTSD from his time in Afghanistan. He told me all about it."

"Yeah I bet he did," Thomas snapped. He looked jealous again and Bianca couldn't help but notice. She smiled inside, thinking how good it was to get some of her own back.

"We need to get a closer look, I need to see what he's doing in there."

"The man is probably having a drink, Bianca."

"Yeah but who with, and why? Thomas, this is really weird. First Gary and now Brad. It's getting stranger by the minute, don't you think?"

"Okay yeah, it is a bit strange. Honestly, I didn't think much about it regarding Gary, but since you studied this Brad fellow too, I'm starting to wonder..."

"About time," Bianca retorted. "Come on, you were in the police for long enough. Surely this is a weird situation worthy of investigation."

"I was never a detective, Bianca. I was an action guy. I might be good at pretexting, but I'll admit I'm not particularly good at detective work." Bianca thought this was a strange comment to make, considering that she had always believed the two to go hand-in-hand.

She sat there with the cool breeze blowing across her face. Her eyes were zoomed in on The Columbian. She suddenly broke her own silence, "Hey, what are we doing? Fuck, we're stupid. You can just wander in there. If Gary is in there, it doesn't matter. He doesn't know he was your subject and that you've been reassigned. Just go in there and see what Brad is up to."

Thomas couldn't say no. She was right, he could just walk in and continue as if he was back on the job. It might actually impress Bianca, he thought, to see him in action for herself.

"Um, what did you say Brad looked like again?"

Bianca rolled her eyes behind her Christian Diors. "He's wearing the navy-blue jacket, blue jeans with tan boots. He has really dark short hair, almost black, and brown eyes. *Really* good looking."

"*Really* good looking?" Thomas repeated.

"Not as good as you, baby." Bianca pulled her sunglasses down onto her nose, revealing her eyes. She fluttered them at him. Thomas melted a little inside. He felt silly for feeling jealous. She most assuredly only had eyes for him.

Bianca watched as Thomas jaywalked across the road, and was narrowly missed by a car. *Cops,* she thought, *do as I say, not as I do.*

Bianca was dying to find out what Thomas had seen. She had been waiting at the coffee shop by herself for over an hour, and considering that she and Thomas had already been there a few hours prior, she felt she may have been outstaying the café's hospitality.

The emo-looking waitress who had earlier brought them their coffees and lunch came up to her. "You want another coffee?"

"Actually, are you licensed? If so, I'll have a wine. After looking over all this work, I think I deserve it." Bianca waved her hand over the papers that were now clipped together in neat little bundles. The waitress smiled. She had a pretty smile. Bianca thought it a shame that the girl probably only busted it out twice a year.

As the wine appeared on the table in front of her, Bianca saw Gary Stephenson walk out of the pub and down the street. Shortly after that Brad Saunders walked out of the bar too. He headed off in the same direction as Gary, keeping a good distance between himself and Gary. About five minutes later Bianca watched as Thomas once again jaywalked across the busy street. He managed to make it back to their table in one piece.

"You really should cross the road in the legally prescribed

manner, you know. You almost got yourself killed." Thomas thought how much Bianca sounded like his mother.

"It's all good, nothing happened to me."

"Maybe not then, but something could..."

"Ha, unlikely." He noticed Bianca had ordered herself a wine. He was starting to think that maybe the woman did have a drinking problem. Thomas took a seat back in his chair.

"I just saw Gary leave followed by Brad. What happened in there?"

Bianca still had her sunglasses on. She had pushed them all the way back up, and Thomas couldn't see her eyes. He hated not being able to see them. "In my expert opinion, Brad is studying Gary."

Both sat there in silence. Thomas knew he was right. He had only observed the man's movements for an hour or so, but Brad seemed to go about things the same way as himself. He was unquestionably covert, but not covert enough for someone who was looking for it.

Thomas broke the silence. "What type of messed up pile of shit are we in?" He looked around, leaning in and lowering his voice. "Surely The Agency doesn't not trust all its employees to the point that they have us all spying on each other? He leaned back. "This is fucked up."

Bianca nodded her head in agreement and said, "Let's pack up now. We need to get out of here. Meet me at my apartment."

CHAPTER 21

Outer Eastern Suburbs, Melbourne, Victoria

B ACK AT THE APARTMENT, for the first time Bianca and Thomas were not on the lounge, but sitting up at the kitchen bench. They also didn't have any alcohol in front of them. Thomas thought Bianca must be feeling sick.

Bianca had that outer-space stare on her face again. Thomas broke her out of it. "As I said at the café, this is totally fucked up. What is going on?" He paused momentarily then continued without giving Bianca a chance to reply. "Look, I know I doubted you when you questioned me studying Gary, but after what I just saw I have no doubt that Brad is some type of spook. If he is a member of The Agency too, then Agency employees are being told to study their own." He shook his head in disbelief and confusion.

"What do we call our jobs, Thomas?"

Thomas looked at her blankly. Bianca continued, "I mean, what we call a person we are sourcing information from?"

"A subject."

"Correct. And what do we call it instead of 'spying'?"

"Information acquirement," he immediately replied.

"No, not usually. You said it just before; we generally call it 'studying', don't we?"

"True, we do. What are you getting at, Bianca?" Thomas asked, trying to see what was going on inside the woman's brain. Over the past week he had realised how much smarter than him she was. But he couldn't let her know that. Her head was already as inflated as a hot air balloon and at times he felt he would have liked to prick it with a needle. He thought how lucky she was that it was such a pretty head.

Bianca looked around the kitchen. She saw Samson asleep on the balcony. True to its reputation, the weather had changed and the sun was now back out from behind the clouds and the wind had stopped.

"Thomas, all I've ever done all my life is take orders. Yes sir, no sir, you want to fuck my arse, sir?"

Thomas raised his eyebrows at her.

Bianca continued. "I rarely question anything and I do what I'm told in regard to my work. I've always had faith in the 'need to know' system. I always believed that if I needed to be told I would be, and if I'm not told then it's of no concern to me." Bianca's gaze swept across the bench looking for her glass of wine, then she remembered she didn't have one. "I've been with The Agency for three years now and I've never questioned any of the jobs or why the clients want such information, or even the need for the ridiculous wellness checks for that matter. But

I'm questioning now!"

Thomas deliberated on Bianca's words. *'Fuck my arse, sir?'* *Shit*, he thought, *she sure was a compliant girl.*

"So what do you think is really going on?"

"They have us studying each other, Thomas."

"Yeah, I know that, I said that before. They don't trust us."

"No, you're looking at it from one angle only. Think a bit more laterally. They have us studying each other, not because they don't trust us, but for some other reason."

"No, no way. That makes zero sense. Why would they want to do that?"

"I don't fucking know!" Bianca snapped. She really wanted a drink but she hadn't felt well after the wine at the café. Her lunch must be playing up on her. "Well, I could take a stab and say they want to find out what we do, how we react, what we say, maybe what we will do for them..?"

"That still doesn't make any sense. If we're all running around studying each other, then where is the money coming from? Subjects studying each other doesn't make any money for the business."

"Maybe North Korea, Thomas. They fund everything else," Bianca said half joking, half thinking that maybe she was on to something.

Thomas ignored the North Korea comment, thinking it ridiculous. "How can they make money if there is no real client? They pay us well... well, I don't know about you, but I get paid a fairly hefty sum."

Bianca didn't like the tone he took when he said that. She

decided not to leave that one aside, and retaliated, "You said that as if I'd be paid less than you because I'm a woman."

Thomas didn't back down. "I'm on over $100 an hour."

"Same." Bianca retorted.

Thomas didn't say anything. He decided to get back to the main conversation instead of expending energy on a frivolous tangent that Bianca obviously didn't think was frivolous.

"Bianca, I know I saw what I saw and I believe you about Gary and Brad, but I don't know if we have enough evidence to back your theory that we're all subjects in some fucked-up science experiment funded by the Workers' Party of Korea."

"What? I never said that. You're putting words in my mouth. I just said it adds up to the fact they have agency employees studying each other. I didn't say that we were part of some weird experiment, but now..." she paused and Thomas could see those cogs of hers were working overtime. "That actually kinda makes sense." Once again Bianca went to reach for a glass that wasn't there.

"Here, I'll get you a drink," said Thomas.

"No, sit down, I'm fine. We need to work this out."

Thomas scratched his head. He looked as though his brain was going to implode any second. He felt like it too. He couldn't remember being this confused since Amy Jacobs had stood him up for a date at high school.

"Well even if we're right about the science experiment theory, it still doesn't answer who is funding and why."

"Could be Donald Trump."

Thomas didn't laugh at Bianca's attempt at a joke. In the

military she had always been told to maintain a sense of humour. She guessed they didn't enforce that in police training.

"My God, I just had a thought. The Agency is now ordering terminations, correct?"

Thomas nodded his head in agreement. "Yeah, well they asked me to terminate you..."

"That's right. I'm on the hit list - and Lord forbid, you could be on it too! Thomas, they could have some other Agency employee onto you and you don't even know it!" Bianca wrapped her arms around him, reaching out from her seat. She squeezed him tightly.

Thomas squeezed her back then released his grasp and said: "Fuck me, if you're right then this is one of the most fucked-up things I've ever heard of." Thomas now felt that he needed a drink of Jack or Jim.

"You're not wrong, the whole thing is insane. But we aren't insane. I mean, I know I'm not. The more you think about it, the more it makes sense."

Thomas couldn't help but agree with her. The more he thought about it the more it did make sense. There were many things that The Agency did that he thought were strange or really weren't necessary, but just like Bianca he hadn't questioned it. He was starting to feel that he had just been some type of submissive at their beck and call. He put his head in his hands. "If we are correct, then why did they pick us? Why did they recruit us for The Agency?"

Bianca shook her head. Her brain was a complete cluster at the moment. She felt she needed something stronger than a drink.

Unfortunately, none of that type of stuff was on hand. Suddenly she realised that all her subjects were just like each other, and in many ways, just like her. One thing that had always stuck in her mind, and she had thought strange, was that they all seemed to have experienced some traumatic event in their life.

"Thomas, you said you knew that Gary Stephenson's wife and daughter had been murdered by an armed intruder one night while he was away on secondment in the UK with BAE Systems?"

"Yeah. Well I told you I knew about the murders. I knew the other as well, though, because it was in his job file. Why do you ask?" Thomas was intrigued. He could tell the woman was going somewhere with this.

"Well, don't you think it's unusual that all of us - you, me, Gary and Brad - well, we all had some type of trauma happen to us before being involved with The Agency? I mean, you with the siege, Gary with the murders, Brad with what happened in Afghanistan, me with the ..." Bianca's voice faded off.

"You with the what? Bianca, what happened to you?"

Bianca's demeanour changed and her Berlin Wall was back up and stronger than ever. "I prefer not to talk about it."

"Come on, if what we are surmising is true, then you've been studied too." Bianca suddenly shuddered as she realised that she may have been a subject too. She started racking her brain, trying to think who could have been onto her, as she really didn't have that much to do with people. Realistically she tried to avoid them for the most part, except when she was on the job, of course.

"No, actually I've never spoken to anyone about it. Obviously the other Agency employees are not as good as me." She immediately realised what she had said and saw by the look on Thomas's face that he had taken it to heart. She decided not to apologise as it was the truth, and he would just have to deal with it.

Thomas did quickly deal with Bianca's indirect stab at him by deciding to drop trying to find out what had happened to her. He may not be quite as smart as her, but he was a good operator and he knew he'd be able to get it out of her at some point.

"Come on, Bianca, do you really think that The Agency was behind those events you mentioned? That's way too far-fetched!"

"You are asking leading questions. No wonder you were never a detective!" said Bianca, starting to be exasperated with the man. But she caught herself and pulled herself back into line. "No," she said softly, gazing into Thomas's blue eyes, thinking they looked like a sky on a crystal-clear day. "Of course I don't think The Agency or whoever is funding them, was behind those events. Shit happens. I do think, though, that maybe we were all picked to work for The Agency because of those events." Bianca paused and looked almost thoughtful. "They are picking people who were fucked, are fucked or fucked up."

Thomas deliberated on her comment. He then slammed his fist down on the kitchen bench. It made Samson wake up and he came racing through the kitchen and into the living area. "I'm going to freaking kill someone, hey!"

Thomas's sudden physical outburst had scared Bianca almost as much as it had Samson. She regained her composure. "Look, baby, I know you're mad. So am I. We need to calm ourselves down, look at what we know and go from there."

Bianca went to one of the kitchen drawers and pulled out some sheets of butcher's paper and a couple of marker pens. She spread the paper out across the kitchen bench, but not before putting down some placemats to protect her Caesar stone.

Always thinking, that girl, Thomas thought. *Maybe even a bit too much.*

Bianca started scribbling away on the paper. She wrote her name, when she had started at The Agency, the name of all her subjects and their basic backgrounds. Thomas followed suit. The pair compared their notes and found that Gary Stephenson was not the only overlap.

"Richie too? Bianca, he's old enough to be your Dad!" Thomas exclaimed as they discovered the crossover in subjects they'd studied.

"Yeah, well, so is Daniel Craig, but I'd let him shit on me."

Thomas looked at the woman speechless. He'd loved her filthiness in the bedroom but that was just going too far.

Bianca continued, "This is enough evidence for me. We need to stop this right now. I'm not going to be someone's subject."

CHAPTER 22

South Melbourne, Victoria

"I WAS MORE THAN pleased to receive your text," said Cheryl, holding Bianca's chin between her fingers. She moved the chin from side to side, looking for a sign of a turkey neck.

"Your neck is still acceptable, but at some point in time you will need to have some type of lift done."

"I understand," Bianca uttered, deciding to just comply. She was also having trouble speaking with her chin and jaw being held in the position it was. She rolled her eyes over to the side of the room. David had entered into her wellness check about five minutes ago, unannounced. Cheryl hadn't even bothered to look up from the inspection when he had come in and taken a seat. He was tapping away again on his Surface Pro, randomly looking up at the women from time to time.

A one-man audience for The Bianca show again, Bianca thought.

Cheryl ran her eyes over her subject's left arm. "What's this bruise on your wrist?"

Cheryl's phone beeped. Bianca couldn't help hearing it, given her boss was so close to her. Bianca knew it was Thomas. He was right on cue.

"Excuse me, Bianca. I'll be back shortly."

"No probs."

Bianca waited until Cheryl was completely out of the examination room before she headed over to where David was sitting. Bianca was topless and only had on her panties. This time, though, they weren't her practical type.

Bianca sat on the desk where David was typing away. He immediately closed the screen of the Surface Pro. He admired the woman, who was as close to him as she had ever been. He had to stop himself from putting his face straight into her bare breasts there and then.

"David?"

"Yes, Bianca?" he said, staring at her chest.

"Before you came in, Cheryl told me that I had a new subject, Gary Stephenson. I haven't been given a job file yet, though. Are you preparing it for me?" She fluttered her doe eyes at him.

"Well that's strange, I thought Gary Stephenson was already being studied by another employee. Cheryl must have changed her mind."

"Yeah - she must have. She said the client wanted as much information as I could get, especially in relation to his work with weapons technology and his time with BAE Systems."

Bianca leaned in closer. One of her nipples was almost poking David's eye out. He kind of wished it would have a better go at it.

"David?"

"Yes, Bianca?" He was using every ounce of control not to wrap his mouth around one of her breasts and start sucking on it like an infant.

"How long have you been employed here again? I forget." Bianca gave him a smile.

David smiled back at her, thinking it was no wonder she was his favourite subject. "I was employed not long after you started, I believe. I took over from Alex."

"Yeah, Alex. He was great," Bianca got off the desk and walked to the corner of the room. She picked up her pile of clothes and walked out of the examination room.

David called out to her, "Hey, where are you going?"

"I need to go to the bathroom, I have my period."

David scrunched his nose up. Despite his PhDs, he still couldn't believe that a creature could bleed for five days and not die. It was just unnatural.

Cheryl re-entered the room. She had been in her sound-proof office talking with Thomas and the conversation had gone down better than expected. Cheryl was pleasantly surprised by her subject and his willingness.

"Where is she?"

"Who?" David asked stupidly.

"Bianca of course! Where did she go?"

"She's in the bathroom, she has her rags."

"No she doesn't." Cheryl knew Bianca's menstrual cycle inside and out.

Beep. It was Cheryl's phone again. She looked at it and saw it was Bianca. She read the text: *So sorry - I was not feeling well at all, I had to leave. I'll let you know when I'm feeling better.*

Cheryl was not impressed. Bianca was never sick. She texted back: *You better be dying to leave like that. Let me know when you are better ASAP.*

"David, that was Bianca. Apparently she isn't feeling well."

"What about her wellness check? You were hardly even half way through," David said in a disappointed tone.

"Well, I just heard from Thomas, and you may be interested in the conversation..."

Her prepaid phone wasn't as snazzy as her Samsung, but it would have to do. She rang Thomas's new number. They had gone and bought the new phones together and exchanged numbers.

"Bianca?"

She liked the sound of his voice. It was calming amongst the chaos that seemed to be engulfing her life.

"Yep. Thank you, Thomas, your text was right on cue."

"Not a problem, I told her just as we discussed. We've bought ourselves some time."

"So she thinks you're going to do it, then."

"Yep."

There was silence down the line. Suddenly Thomas spoke. "Bianca, since you didn't like my suggestion, we need to work out a proper plan."

"I already have one."

"You do?"

"I do, but you need to come to the country with me for a few days. It's now vital."

"I thought you'd just wanted me to come to do you a favour?"

"That was the plan, but just like any good plan one should be able to adapt it to the changing situation."

Once again there was silence. Thomas recognised the words Bianca had just spoken. They had been his words to her in what now seemed a lifetime ago, even though it had only been a few weeks. Thomas hadn't wanted to go away to the country with her then, but that was only because he didn't want to give her the wrong impression and lead her on about status of their relationship. However, the situation now changed everything. If going to the country with her was now vital to the plan, he'd do it. He would just have to trust her.

"I'll come, just let me know when."

"We'll leave tomorrow. Be at mine by 9am. We'll be away for two nights."

"Tony, *Zio*."

"Yes, I'm on a new number."

"I'm well. I'll be there tomorrow afternoon."

"Yes *Zio*, I'm still bringing Samson and my friend. I just have a bit more of a favour to ask you.

"Yes, yes, I'm still wanting that, but now I also need something else. Do you still have that 50 Cal?"

It shall be like living among scorpions

Ezekiel 2:6

CHAPTER 23

Hume Highway, North East Victoria

"I STILL CAN'T BELIEVE you brought the cat," said Thomas, looking at Samson curled up on the backseat of his own 4WD. Bianca had let the cat straight out of its carry cage and onto the leather seats as soon as they had climbed into the vehicle.

Thomas had volunteered that they take his Range Rover as he'd concluded it was a hell of a lot more comfortable then being cramped up in that bubble car of hers. He just didn't know that Samson would be coming along for the ride.

"I couldn't leave him at home. He would have been lonely."

"He's a cat, Bianca. As long as you left out plenty of water and biscuits, he would have been fine for two days."

"You obviously don't have a pet, do you?" she retaliated.

"No, I don't. I don't have the time and I don't particularly want one. I have enough on my hands as it is."

"Naturally," Bianca commented, referring to Thomas's wife and children.

Thomas knew what Bianca's comment meant. He had picked up on her subtle way of speaking between the lines sometimes.

"Why couldn't you have just had someone look after him?"

"I don't trust many people ... to look after him, that is."

Thomas rolled his eyes. He'd just have to put up with the cat in the car, he guessed. He decided to send Samson a mind message: *If you even think about putting one of those claws into my leather, I'll be making a stole out of you.* Samson continued purring away on the backseat.

Something had been on Thomas's mind since the other day at Bianca's apartment. Actually, lots of things had been on his mind, but his curiosity was beginning to get the better of him. He suddenly spoke. "So as I have agreed to come out here with you, and I've trusted you that this is all part of some great plan of yours, I only feel it is fair you divulge a little more about yourself to me without us having to play the usual games."

Bianca pondered on his request. She decided to let her guard down. She thought how she didn't have anything to lose anyway.

"Ok, so what exactly would you like to know about me?"

"Everything," Thomas answered.

For a moment, Bianca felt very wanted and she blushed. Despite this feeling, she knew she would never tell him 'everything.'

"Well, you know that's not going to happen Thomas. What do you want to know the most?"

"I want to know what happened to you. I mean I want to know why you think The Agency may have recruited you."

"Because I'm exceptional," Bianca laughed.

Thomas looked slightly annoyed. He thought how the woman never seemed to stop playing the game.

Bianca noticed the look. "Okay, okay. You want to know what happened to me? Well here it is. I used to be in the ADF and during my service I was raped. I mean I was really quite brutally gang raped by a few guys I worked with. It put me in hospital. They discharged me not long after."

"Oh baby, I'm so sorry," Thomas said suddenly feeling guilty of how rough he had been with her.

"Nothing to be sorry about Thomas. What doesn't kill you only makes you stronger."

Bianca had easily come to terms with the event. Her family's promise had made it all easier to deal with also. She remembered the big smile she had had on her face when she had read the ADF media release on the sudden deaths of two RAAF personnel.

"So what did you end up telling your wife, anyway?" asked Bianca noticeably changing the subject of conversation. Thomas couldn't help but hear the jealous undertone.

"Just told her I'd be catching up with an old VICPOL mate who's going to help me with the book."

"And she believed that?" Bianca asked with wide eyes.

"Yeah, well I'm here with you, aren't I?" Thomas indicated left and changed lanes. "I'm going to pull over here, we need to top up." Thomas pulled the Range Rover over at a service station that resembled a miniature town. There was a Hungry Jacks, an Oliver's and something that tried too hard to look like a Melbourne café. There was also a park area with its own toilets.

"Here, take this," Bianca said as she pushed a wad of cash towards Thomas.

Thomas laughed, "Don't insult me."

Bianca put the cash back in her purse. "Fine, but you gotta use cash."

Fuck me, Thomas thought. *Sometimes the woman really does treat me like I'm a complete imbecile.*

Thomas got back into the car after paying for the fuel. He threw two Snickers Bars into the centre console.

"Really?" Bianca asked looking at the chocolates.

"Hey, I'm hungry okay, and they had a two-for-one deal. You can have one if you like."

"Thanks, but no thanks," she said with disgust. The mere thought of eating such processed and refined sugars made her stomach squirm on her best days, and at the moment her stomach was still not feeling right.

They headed back down the highway before taking an exit.

"So how much further is the property from here?" Thomas asked.

"We've got a couple of hours to go yet. Oh yeah, and I may have forgotten to mention there isn't much reception out there."

"What? I will need to call Jody at some point, you know?" Thomas said abrasively, thinking about the multiple mobiles he had on him and the women he needed to contact while away.

"It's okay, if you walk up a particular hill and stand on one leg and stick your tongue out, then you might be able to pick up a signal." Bianca was laughing at her own joke. She couldn't help visualising him actually doing it.

"I hope you're joking."

Bianca continued to laugh, "Of course I am, stop being so serious! Look, reception is just in and out, I'm sure you will be able to make a call."

"Well that's okay then. Wow, you were right, we are going bush." Thomas noticed the changing landscape and thought how clean his Range Rover currently was. He hoped the property wasn't on a dirt road, but somehow he knew it would be.

Great, he thought, *my car is not only going to be full of fur and have scratch marks, but it's going to be covered in dust as well. She's just lucky she's such a good fuck.*

"So let's talk about your plan," said Thomas, changing his line of thought. "Here we are in the middle of bum-fuck-nowhere, with your cat, and you still haven't told me jack shit."

"You'll find out when we get to my uncle's, okay? You just need to have some faith in me. Take a chill pill."

Thomas looked over at Bianca, who was relaxing back into the passenger seat. She looked as if she had taken a chill pill. She appeared very calm, even more so than usual. Thomas made a note of how he would have to check the vehicle for any of her long brunette strands of hair, as his wife had blonde hair.

"Your uncle's, hey? So he has a farm or something out here?"

"Yeah that's right. Him and my aunt. Antonio and Margaret are their names. Well, everyone just calls him Tony. Anyway, they have horses as well as ducks and chickens plus plenty of other interests to keep them occupied."

Horses? Thomas thought. He cringed. Thomas was afraid of horses. He'd disliked them with a passion ever since he was made to go trail riding when he was a child and the beast had taken off, resulting in him landing on the ground and suffering a severely broken leg.

"I don't have to go riding, do I?" he asked.

"Horse riding? No. I mean, you can if you want, but this trip is now more of a business trip." Bianca paused, dissecting what he had actually said. "What? You don't want to go horse riding?"

"No, I hate horses."

What the fuck was wrong with the man? He didn't seem to be much of a cat lover, and now horses! Bianca decided to bite her tongue and not let her disapproval show. They hadn't had sex for a couple of days and Bianca was starting to get toey despite her upset gut.

"That's okay, baby, each to their own. You don't have to go anywhere near the horses." She put her hand on his leg and gave it a gentle rub.

"Good," Thomas replied. "You know you've asked a lot of me already. Most men wouldn't do this much."

Bianca's eyes had been closed but now she opened them and turned her head towards Thomas while still keeping it rested against the seat.

"Excuse me? What are you saying? Are you saying that most men in your position would have just killed me as asked and then gone back to their wife and family as if I'd never existed? Is that what you're saying?"

Thomas heard the disdain in her voice. She really sounded pissed. He hated it when she was like this, but at the same time found it oddly sexy.

"I don't know, Bianca. I don't know what most men would have done in my position, I'm not most men."

Oh, but yes you are, Thomas, Bianca thought to herself.

Somewhere in North East Victoria

"Bianca...*ciao cara!*" Tony said, walking over to his favourite niece. He wrapped his arms around her and gave her a big hug and a kiss on either cheek.

"*Zio, come stai? Questo è Thomas,*" Bianca said, waving her hand towards Thomas, who was standing a few metres back. She beckoned him forward.

Thomas walked up to the man, who appeared to be sizing him up. He had on a pair of dirty jeans and an old workwear shirt. His RM Williams boots had clearly seen better days. Thomas put out his hand to greet the man, but instead Tony grabbed him and pulled him in, giving him a kiss on either cheek as he had with Bianca. Thomas was surprised by the move, having never been kissed by a guy before, apart from when he was a child.

"Ah Bianca, you made it! It's so good to see you!" declared Margaret with a big smile on her face, as she wiped her hands on her apron. She grabbed Bianca and kissed her cheeks.

Margaret looked Thomas up and down. Thomas felt like the woman was checking him out, analysing if he was up to standard for Bianca. Thomas couldn't help but notice the size of the Aunt's breasts. She had a huge rack on her, and she was okay for an old duck too.

"Hi Margaret. This is Thomas, my friend..."

Friend? Thomas pondered, *that was an interesting use of words. Well, I guess she couldn't say lover, now could she? That just would have been awkward.*

"Hi Thomas, so pleased to meet you. I'm so glad you came with Bianca. Welcome to our farm."

Margaret came into Thomas's personal space and gave him a kiss on either cheek just as her husband had done. He could feel the woman's breasts rub right up against his chest.

"That's okay, thanks for having me. The air sure feels clean out here," Thomas commented. He had his nose in the air sniffing like a dog on a scent. The air was clean and cold, and the grass the brightest green he had ever laid eyes on. Thomas could hear the trickle of the creek that ran through the property. In the distance a horse neighed. Goose bumps suddenly rose upon his skin.

"Yep mate, it certainly is. This is God's country. I don't know how you city folk do it. Couldn't think of anything worse. All that pollution and noise... and the traffic. My word, don't even get me started on the traffic."

Bianca butted in, half laughing. "Word of advice, Thomas. When Tony says not to get him started on something, best not to get him started on it." Bianca looked over at her uncle, who had a grin on his face.

"Why Bianca, whatever do you mean, my dear?" he asked, acting stupid.

"Ha, you know exactly what I mean, *Zio.*"

Private joke, Thomas thought. He did feel a bit out of place standing there. This wasn't his usual environment at all, and his now dust-covered navy-blue desert boots were completely impractical. It was the first time he had spent time with a family outside his own, and moreover they seemed to be speaking in Italian a bit too. He hoped they wouldn't be chatting away in their native tongue the whole time they were there. As much as he liked hearing Bianca's sexy accent, people speaking in another language in front of those who couldn't understand, was to him utterly rude and one of his pet hates.

"Come on in, you two," ordered Margaret.

Thomas grabbed their bags out of the vehicle and Bianca put Samson in his cage and carried him towards the house.

Margaret looked at Tony as she walked with him back towards the farmhouse, allowing Bianca and Thomas to go ahead. "The chooks are in, aren't they?"

"Yep, don't worry; they're safe in their pen."

Margaret looked relieved. "Good, because we have a show coming up soon."

Margaret had really laid on a feast for them. There was an assortment of breads with oils to dip into, cold meats and some side dishes Thomas had never even heard of before. The aunt had also made a chicken cacciatore that was just delicious. He was pretty impressed considering that Margaret wasn't even Italian herself. He guessed that's what you got when you married into an Italian family. He thought someone put in that position would either sink or swim, and Margaret appeared to be a natural swimmer - or maybe it was just that her large breasts kept her afloat?

"Thank you, Margaret. That was awesome, especially the *cacciatore*," Thomas said showing off his social graces once again.

"You are more than welcome," said Margaret, sounding pleased with herself. She looked over at her husband as if to say *See? See what a good cook I am?*

Tony ignored his wife's look and instead questioned Thomas. "You know what *cacciatore* means, don't you?"

"No, sorry I don't," he replied, feeling a little ashamed of his ignorance, and never having taking any interest in any language other than English.

"It means 'hunter' in Italian. Isn't that right, Bianca?"

Bianca glared at her uncle. She was surprised her uncle had even brought that up. She turned her attention to Thomas, who seemed interested in her answer. "It certainly does."

Margaret looked disapprovingly at the remaining food on Bianca's plate. "My girl, you are much too skinny, have some more." Margaret shoved some bread towards her niece's face.

"No, Margaret, I'm fine thank you. It was truly delicious

though; I'm just so full," she said, rubbing her bloated tummy.

Tony decided he would try his hand at getting something else down the woman's throat. He knew her vice.

"Maybe some more *vino* then?" he said as he poured the alcohol into Bianca's glass.

"That's enough, thank you" she said, putting her hand out.

Odd, Thomas thought, *Bianca was usually a fish.*

"Well, I'm sure Thomas will have some more, and after we finish this bottle, he can help me with the grappa."

"Grappa? Is that the one that's homemade?" Thomas questioned.

"Can be. I make my own. Rocket fuel, my stuff. I could probably sell it to Boeing."

Thomas laughed and so did Bianca. He looked at her and saw how beautiful she looked sitting there, her skin glowing. It was just how it had looked in the café not long after he'd met her. Thomas also couldn't help but notice how happy she seemed to be. Unlike him, she had surprisingly fit right into the country environment.

"Tony, don't get the boy too drunk now. He won't forgive you for the hangover he'll have," said Margaret.

"Don't worry, Margaret, I can hold my own," Thomas immediately replied, not wanting to appear a pussy.

"That sounds like a challenge, then." Tony had a big smile on his face, excited to have a drinking partner for the night, or at least part of it. He knew Thomas would only make a few rounds before passing out. He chuckled inside, thinking about the city slicker curled up like a baby on the floor.

"You are in for it now, you can't back out of this one," Bianca said, and she laughed her nervous little laugh.

"Oh, I won't be backing out." As he said this, Thomas shot Bianca a look that said: *When are you going to let me in on the plan - why the fuck are we here?*

Bianca read the look straight away. "Zio, would you like to tell Thomas about some of your beliefs?"

"Why certainly, which one?"

"Maybe start with the zombie apocalypse."

Zombie apocalypse? What the fuck? Who were these crazies? It seemed to Thomas that someone had been watching way too much of *The Walking Dead*. But he thought he'd better play along with it, as they sounded half serious.

"What about the zombie apocalypse?" he asked, trying not to sound facetious.

"Well my friend, let's just say we are more than prepared for it."

CHAPTER 25

South Melbourne, Victoria

"HAVE YOU HEARD FROM Bianca yet? Is she feeling better?"

"No David, I haven't heard anything from her."

"Well, are you going to follow up? She's been off the job for a few days now."

"Don't you worry, sick or not, that girl is always on the job," Cheryl stated with a smile, thinking how well she knew her subject.

"Well I doubt she is out and about on the street studying Subject 002 if she isn't well, especially in this weather. She might be good, but she's not a machine, Cheryl. She's getting older too, she has her limits."

"I'm sorry?" Cheryl asked almost choking on her water. "What do you mean 'studying subject 002?' Subject 002 was assigned to Brad Saunders. You know that."

Fuck, thought David. *Fuck, fuck, fuck*. He lowered his head and sat in silence. He knew this would result in an absolute face ripping by Cheryl.

"What the hell is going on, David?"

"Well, the other day during Bianca's wellness check..."

"Yes. I'm waiting."

"Well, you went out of the room and she asked me if I was preparing her job file for her newest subject, Gary Stephenson. She said you had told her she was going to be studying him."

Cheryl raised her perfect eyebrow. The woman didn't look furious; she just looked as if she was still trying to deliberate on the information.

"Hmph," was all that eventually come out of the boss's mouth. She grabbed her water bottle and took a seat, then took a big drink from the stainless steel container.

"And what did you say?"

"Um, well, I said I thought you already had another employee doing that job."

"And then what happened?"

"That's when she left."

This was it, David was preparing to have his arse torn anew. Surprisingly, Cheryl was non-reactive.

"Well, David, this is very odd indeed. Do you know why this is odd?

David shook his head.

"It's odd because Bianca has already studied Gary. Gary was one of her first subjects when she started. Before you joined The Agency project, actually."

"Oh, I had forgotten that," he said, flicking his mind back through the briefings he'd received when he took over from Alex.

"Obviously," stated Cheryl, so calmly it was scaring David.

Cheryl was right, he thought to himself. *For someone so smart I truly can be stupid at times.*

Cheryl continued, "Well, it looks like I have a phone call to Canberra to make. This changes everything."

"How do you mean?" asked David, feeling stupider by the minute.

"Well, David, she's got more of a mind of her own then we all gave her credit for. We also need to find out what she knows, since this could take the study in a whole new direction." David noticed that Cheryl seemed very pleased with herself, but couldn't help feeling his boss was holding something from him.

"What? You think she might actually know about The Agency?" David looked horrified at the thought.

"Highly unlikely, but it can't be ruled out. However, Subject 008 is the real problem at hand. The only reason Bianca knows Gary is back on the books is because he has said something to her and she's recognised the name. The man is fucking hopeless at holding his tongue. I'm going to text him and tell him that he'll be reassigned."

"Who will you reassign him to?" asked David, thinking that there weren't any more subjects left without getting a double-up. The Department had put a hold on presenting possible candidates for the role since the new government had come in and gone all tight-arsed on them.

Cheryl shook her head at him. "He won't end up being reassigned because he will be dead."

Somewhere in North East Victoria

"He's out cold."

"Oh Tony, I told you not to do it to him," Margaret flapped like a mother hen.

"He'll be right, Margaret, just wait and see," said Bianca lovingly, looking at Thomas, who had passed out on the couch with a big bottle of grappa still sitting in front of him on the coffee table.

"Sleeping like a baby," Tony uttered. "Come on, Bianca, I have some things for you."

The pair walked out of the living area, leaving Margaret to finish cleaning up the bottles and glasses. They made their way out to a large shed and Bianca stood back as Tony fiddled with what appeared to be a thousand locks before the door of the armoury opened.

Tony entered another code into a large safe and pulled out a concealable combination knife and ballistics vest.

"Here you go, try it on for size."

Bianca took off her cable knit sweater and put the vest on. It fitted snuggly around her small frame.

"Yep, feels good on. *Grazie, Zio.*"

"I'm glad, because it's the best on the market - made by The Best Bulletproof Vest."

Bianca started to laugh.

"No, seriously, that's the name of the manufacturer. It can withstand all spike, stab and edge bladed weapons. Also, of course, most small arms fire, and it's rated NıJı11 and exceeds US government and military requirements." Tony bent down and pulled out another case. "I also have the silencer you asked about. It's the new SilencerCo Hybrid 46 model. Now, this will fit onto a multitude of different handguns, from your beloved Beretta 92SF up to an H&K USP45."

Tony grabbed a case out of the safe and pulled out a Sig P226 Combat chambered in 9mm. "Now, to fit the silencer, all you have to do is..."

Bianca interrupted him. "It's okay. I know how to fit the piece."

"Oh Bianca, I'm sure you do; but just let me show you, you know, for peace of mind. I wouldn't want anything happening to you. You're my favourite niece, you know?"

Bianca smiled at her uncle. He really did love her.

"Ok, I'm watching."

"Well, first remove the barrel thread, then line up the threads of the silencer and turn clockwise. Once it gets near the end of the thread you just need to align the silencer so you get a full sight picture, then tighten the nut on the silencer by hand."

Bianca watched intently as her uncle fitted the silencer to the Sig pistol and then removed it. She admired how well drilled his actions were, not clumsy and slow like hers.

"Bianca, you know I don't like to butt in - unlike the rest of the family - but this time I'm concerned. I have no issues giving you the vest and the silencer, but the 50 Cal? Well, that's a whole other kettle of fish, you know?"

Bianca was silent. She seemed to still be admiring her new pieces of Gucci kit.

"That weapon can take out an armoured vehicle from several kilometres away. You can do serious damage with it."

She stopped admiring her new gifts and looked up at Tony. "That's the whole idea."

Tony shook his head and sighed. "I really hope you know what you're doing. If they catch you, you might as well be the next star on *Orange Is the New Black*. You won't just get done for murder, but they'll probably try to nab you for terrorism too, and if they do that, you are completely fucked. You'll compromise the whole family too, they'll come after us..." Her uncle's voice faded off and Bianca could see how concerned he was, not just for herself, but for the family in general. She thought how much they already had done for her in the past few years since the alleged rape.

Bianca looked at her uncle adoringly, "I won't fuck it up *Zio*, promise. I'll be back here with the weapon before you know it."

"Yeah, I know you will. It's just that I worry about you."

"No need to worry. Like always, I'll be just fine."

Tony looked at his implacable niece. She was nothing like her mother, but everything like him. She really was the son he never had.

"Thomas seemed surprised when I told him about my collection. You obviously hadn't said anything to him, then?"

"You know me, I work on a need-to-know basis. He didn't

need to know until then. He has a bit of a problem keeping his mouth shut sometimes."

"Hmm, I saw that tonight. He was pretty open about telling me some of the things he's been up to and who he's been working for. Sounds like they're all up to something. Sounds like a government conspiracy to me."

"Yeah. I actually may be with you on that one for once," said Bianca, thinking that all his crazy government conspiracy theories didn't sound that crazy at all now.

"Hence the 50 Cal?" asked Tony.

"Hence the 50 Cal."

CHAPTER 26

Somewhere in North East Victoria

"MORNING, SUNSHINE," BIANCA SAID to Thomas, standing over him with a hot coffee. She knew it would be especially strong as Tony had made the pot.

Thomas was struggling to open his eyes. He finally did and looked around the room. It looked like a room that Laura Ashley had thrown up in. He felt like throwing up himself.

"How did I get to bed?" he asked, rubbing his eyes.

Bianca laughed and put down his coffee on the bedside table next to him. "I carried you in here."

"What?" Thomas asked with his eyes still half closed.

"You heard me. I carried you in here and tucked you all up into bed with Mr Tinky." Bianca still had a big grin on her face as she pointed to the soft teddy bear Thomas had held unknowingly for half the night.

Thomas threw the toy on the ground. "Fucking never again."

Bianca couldn't wipe the smile off her face. "Are you referring to sleeping with the teddy or the grappa?"

"Both."

"Ha, Tony is up for round two tonight - you'll have to let him down softly. I think he enjoyed your company. And Mr Tinky, well he can't even look you in the eye after the things he did to you."

Thomas looked at the offending teddy bear and shook his head. "There'll definitely be no round two tonight, I can tell you that right now."

"Well, I was kind of hoping for at least one round tonight; with me, that is. I missed out last night." Thomas knew Bianca wasn't referring to the alcohol.

Thomas gazed at her sitting there on the bed. *The woman even has a sexy way of drinking coffee*, he thought as he admired the cup of the strong liquid on her lips.

"By tonight, I'll be good as good as gold and I'll be able to go *multiple* rounds," he replied with a seductive smile.

Multiple, Bianca repeated to herself inside her head. She liked that word.

"What are the boys doing? Are they out there playing with the toys?"

"Yeah, something like that. I thought I'd just let them have some of their own time."

"I think Tony would like that. He doesn't get to hang around other men too much these days, just me and the horses." Margaret sighed as she looked at herself, thinking the newest filly must have looked more appealing to Tony than herself.

She seemed to be putting on a kilo per minute these days.

"I've got so fat, Bianca."

Bianca looked at her aunt. She hadn't really noticed. Sure, the woman had breasts to rival Dolly Parton's, but overall Bianca thought she still appeared very serviceable.

"Not true. Okay, maybe your breasts have got bigger, but that's not a bad thing, trust me." Bianca thought how much she'd like to slice a piece off each of her Aunt's and attach it to her own.

"Thank you, I just hope Tony still sees it like that … you never do know with men…" her voice faded off.

"Margaret, realistically I don't know much about relationships, but one thing I do know is that the man adores you. He'd do absolutely anything for you." Bianca realised that the truth of the fact was so obvious to her because she had never experienced it herself. With regard to her aunt and uncle's relationship, their unshakable love stood out to her like a sore thumb.

Margaret smiled, feeling a bit better about herself. *Well*, she thought to herself, *I may not be a fancy filly, but I'm not an old nag just yet.*

Bianca's eyes swept around the kitchen systematically. She liked the way all the pots and pans hung on the bracket attached to the ceiling. The whole look was very old school farmhouse. For the most part, she didn't like her aunt's taste in décor -it was much too 1992 for her own liking - but the kitchen she did like. It felt rustic and warm, and Bianca could smell the homemade bread sending mouth-watering wafts through the house. It made her feel all homely inside, as if she might want to start cooking dinner in bare feet instead of her Balmain boots.

"Here, put this on." Margaret threw her a pink and white gingham apron with frills on it. Bianca looked at the garment and wondered if Margaret had made it herself. Without hesitation, she put it on. She didn't want her lambskin vest to be covered in flour.

"I'm going to teach you how to make biscotti, I mean proper biscotti. The one your Nonna made. Your Nonna taught me and now I will teach you. I know your mother hasn't passed it down to you." Margaret felt a little despondent as she said that. It was truly a sad thing to have such a rift in the family, with Bianca and her mother not on speaking terms.

"Here's the recipe for you, the original. It is in Nonna's handwriting and in *Italiano*."

Bianca picked up the piece of paper that was now yellow with age. Nonna's handwriting was a bit of a scribble and the words blurred in front of Bianca's eyes. "Hold on, Margaret," Bianca said. "Let me go get my glasses."

"From what you told me about yourself last night, I understand you are highly trained and experienced on a range of firearms. However, you've never used this, have you?" asked Tony as he opened up the case housing the McMillan Tac-50, a favourite of several militaries around the world. To the side of the case was a large suppressor marked 'AAC Cyclops'.

Thomas was in awe of the weapon. He'd never seen one in real life, and couldn't believe that the firearm was somehow in Bianca's uncle's possession. He finally came out of his awestruck gaze and answered: "That is correct. I tended to use closer-range weapons like the M4 carbine and variants of that, and the H&K MP5 before they took that off us. Even our sniper rifles such as the Accuracy International 308 and Blaser R8 308 had nothing on this. I'm all ears."

"I'm pleased to hear that. Sometimes people in your position can think they know it all. Do you know that this weapon holds the record for longest confirmed sniper kills to date?"

Thomas shook his head at Tony, who continued, "You understand you are going to get one shot at this? If you don't get it right you could end up taking out innocent people. Actually in saying that if you are going to use it as an anti-material rifle, you could still take out innocent people."

Thomas shrugged his shoulders. "Collateral damage," he replied, thinking back to the Sunrise Hotel Siege.

"Good attitude to have. Whatever happens, you have to keep moving forward."

"Completely agree."

"So Thomas, how long have you and Bianca been in a relationship?" Tony asked, completely changing the conversation's tangent.

"We're not in a ..." Thomas caught himself before finishing the sentence. "What I mean is, we haven't known each other for long. It's quite new."

Tony proceeded to pull out the weapon's bipod stand from

the case. He started to unfold it and then attached it to the picatinny rail under the fore-end of the rifle.

"I thought so, by the look of the tan mark on your ring finger."

Thomas looked at his left hand and the finger where he'd taken off his wedding band only the day before. He hadn't thought the white circle of skin it had left behind was noticeable at all, but obviously Tony had exceptional observational skills. It made him wonder what the man had done in a prior life.

"It's okay, mate, you can have a rebound. Just don't do anything to hurt her; she's a precious one."

"She's not the precious type," said Thomas, thinking how the woman could take a pounding.

"That's not what I meant. She is precious to us, *la famiglia*. We would do anything for our Bianca."

Tony returned his attention to the bipod, adjusting the height.

La famiglia - Thomas was sure he'd heard that before, but his Italian was non-existent, apart from *Biancaneve*. He must remember to google the word later.

CHAPTER 27

Somewhere in North East Victoria

B IANCA WAS BENDING OVER looking through the oven door window when Tony and Thomas walked through the farmhouse door. They had obviously finished the lesson.

Bianca hadn't heard a round fired, but she knew that the weapon would have been fitted with a suppressor. She wondered what the hell they had targeted, considering that gun could almost take out the moon. She wasn't too concerned with that now, as long as Thomas was happy he knew how to use it in the correct manner. That would make the job so much more fluid.

Bianca snapped herself back up from her bent position and smiled at Thomas. It was just like the 'bend and snap' the movie *Legally Blonde* had taught her. Thomas stared at the woman. He'd never seen her wearing reading glasses before, and she had on some frilly pink apron. All she needed was pigtails and a thermometer and all his sexual fantasies were alive in front of him.

Thomas walked over to her while Tony took his boots off and proceeded to the bathroom to freshen up. Margaret followed her husband.

Thomas lifted up Bianca's long brunette hair and started to nibble at her neck. He whispered, "I've never seen you wear those glasses before. I like them. You are turning me on."

A tingling sensation went down Bianca's body and she felt Thomas's hardness pressing against her rear. She wished she could just let him prop her up on the kitchen bench there and then, but Tony and Margaret could re-enter the space at any time.

Thomas slid his hand down the front of Bianca's jeans and felt her wetness. He pulled his hand back out and went to put the fingers in his mouth, but instead Bianca grabbed his hand and put them in her own mouth, tasting herself.

This action of self-love turned Thomas on even more and he was just about to lead her down towards the bedroom when one of his phones starting ringing. He pulled the handset out of his pocket and saw it was his wife.

"I'm sorry, I've got to answer this," he said to Bianca.

"That's okay, do what you have to do," she replied.

Thomas answered the call as he made his way outside.

Bianca couldn't help but hear him say, "Hi honey, yep I'm all good. No not much, nothing to get excited about."

Tony and Margaret walked back into the room. They looked a little flustered themselves. Bianca wondered if her uncle had quickly 'freshened' Margaret up.

"Where's Thomas?" Tony asked.

"He's just on a call. He's actually got some reception. How did he go?"

"He should be fine. He's an experienced weapons handler and marksman. I'll be surprised if there is any problem." Margaret walked over and handed him a glass of grappa.

"You want one, Bianca?" She asked.

"God no." Bianca shook her head. "I'll have a *vino*, though."

"Feeling a bit better today, are we?" said Margaret as she poured the red into a glass and handed it to her niece. "You seemed a bit off yesterday."

"Yeah I was bit, but much better today; feel just fine actually." Bianca took a big sip of her favourite substance. "*Zio*, thanks for everything and especially today. I really appreciate the time you spent with Thomas. I can't afford for there to be any problem."

"Anything for you, *cara*. He did, however, ask why you couldn't take the shot?"

"He did?"

"Yeah, he did." Tony downed the rest of his grappa in one hit. He placed the empty glass back on the kitchen bench.

"So what did you tell him?" Bianca asked. She was intrigued to find out his answer.

"Because you're a woman, of course."

The pair laughed and Margaret pretended to not hear the conversation. She had learnt many years ago to just pretend not to hear or see anything. Ignorance was bliss.

Thomas ended his call with Jody. Everything seemed fine at home and she appeared completely oblivious to his actual whereabouts. She had put the children on the phone to him but they only hung on the line for about twenty seconds. They obviously had not yet developed the skills to hold a phone conversation, and in this day and age of texting and social media, he wondered if they ever would.

There were sweet aromas calling him back to the house, and Thomas knew it wasn't just Bianca's honey. However, as he had reception he thought he'd better quickly check his other phones. He looked at his work iPhone. *Crap*, he thought. Cheryl had sent a message ages ago and he hadn't seen it. He read the message and called his boss immediately. As always, her instructions were very clear.

When Thomas finally got off the phone he made his way back to the house and the smells from the oven became stronger.

His lover was sitting up at the kitchen bench still wearing her apron and glasses. He noticed she had a glass of red wine in front of her.

"Back to your old self, I see?" he asked cheekily.

"Certainly am. How about you, how are you feeling?"

"Um, I'm feeling okay now. Not sure if I'm up for a drink yet," he replied, thinking how the rocket fuel had beat him last night. "I'm probably up for a shower, though." Thomas's jeans and woollen jumper were covered in bits of grass from where he had lain in the prone position to fire the weapon.

Bianca surveyed Thomas's face and clothing and agreed that he was looking a bit dirty. *Just the way I like them*, she thought to herself.

Margaret had overhead Thomas and piped up, "I'll get you some fresh towels," as she stopped chopping an onion. Thomas thought it was amazing that the woman didn't even have one tear in her eyes. *Years of experience,* he thought.

Bianca stood up hastily. "No, no, I'll get them," she said, giving Thomas a particular look. Thomas recognised the look immediately and knew he wouldn't be showering alone.

"Make sure you grab the good towels, they're in the linen cupboard, on the second shelf," Margaret called as the pair walked out of the kitchen and down the hall. Bianca stopped at the linen cupboard and grabbed out two soft bath towels, each with an embroidered band around the bottom. The towels smelt like Fab soap powder. They proceeded into the light blue tiled bathroom with a large timber vanity and huge mirror. Bianca shut the door behind them and locked it. Thomas switched on the fan button and then leant in and turned on the shower with the water blasting out almost full bore. Still clothed, he pushed Bianca up against the front of the vanity so she was bent over it facing the mirror. Bianca looked at herself and saw she still had her glasses on. She lifted up her hand to remove them.

"No," said Thomas as he pulled down her jeans revealing the two dimples on her lower back that seemed to be smiling at him. "Leave them on."

Back in the kitchen, Tony was onto his third glass of grappa for the afternoon. Margaret had moved on from the onions and was now rinsing her home-grown green beans.

"So what do you think of Thomas?" she asked her husband.

"I think the man might be fucked," her husband answered, without looking up from the latest edition of *The Land*.

Margaret didn't answer him, but by the way Bianca and Thomas had gone together for a shower, she couldn't help but agree. *Yes, certainly fucked.*

CHAPTER 28

Inner Eastern Suburbs, Melbourne, Victoria

A FTER WHAT SEEMED LIKE the longest drive, Thomas felt real relief to be back home.

Samson had decided to be sick over all his back seat, and the smell of cat vomit had travelled with them all the way back to Melbourne. Also, like someone with severe OCD, Bianca made him repeat every detail of their plan back to her a thousand times. He wasn't used to having to go over a plan again and again. In the SOG, there was never time for that. There was always a plan and you just hoped like hell everyone understood it. He'd got so fed up with her attention to every little detail that he ended up telling her to take a chill pill, just as she had done to him on the way there. Bianca did settle down after that - or maybe she just wanted to try to concentrate on something else, because the next thing Thomas knew, he was receiving head while driving.

As they entered into the outer suburbs of Melbourne, Bianca asked him to pull into a large alcohol chain store, or in her words "Disneyland". He felt obliged, especially after the good job she had done while on the road.

"Why do you call it Disneyland?" he asked her.

"Because it's the happiest place on earth." Thomas laughed and shook his head, thinking *Yeah, the woman really does have a problem*. He, however, grabbed a carton of beer while there as he knew there would probably not be a cold one waiting for him at home.

Thomas carried his bag into the house and in the other hand he held the carton of beer. He put his bag down in the hall and proceeded to the kitchen fridge.

As I suspected, nothing to drink. Lucky I got these, he thought to himself as he put four of the stubbies onto a shelf, struggling to find a space for them in the overcrowded refrigerator.

Jody walked in as he closed the fridge door.

"You're home. I thought you were. Did I hear the vacuum downstairs?"

Shit, he thought. She'd heard him vacuuming out his car, as he had completely forgotten to drop into a carwash on the way back home.

"Yeah honey, I'd bought a packet of chips and when I went to open them, the damn packet exploded!"

His wife laughed. "Yeah well, you wouldn't have liked that. You're so pedantic with your car."

Better to be pedantic than a complete grub, he thought visualising the inside of Jody's BMW. It was such a nice car but

Thomas refused to drive it because the interior resembled a brothel. Over the years he had noticed that females in general just had no respect for their own cars. It was a mystery of life, because if you moved one of the thousand cushions that they all seemed to have adorning their beds and couches, you got ripped a new one, but hey their cars could look like downtown Grozny after the latest bombing and it was a non-issue to them.

"So how did it go? How was Johnno?"

"Yeah, Johnno's good," lied Thomas. "We probably drank too much, though."

"That's what happens when boys get together, I guess. Did he give you some good advice for your book? I heard his is doing well."

"Yeah, he told me writing a book wasn't neurosurgery. Just follow the formula."

"What formula is that?"

"I actually have no idea."

Jody rolled her eyes. She thought it had been strange when Thomas had told her he was planning on writing a novel. He just didn't seem the type. She knew for a fact that her vocabulary and grammatical skills were far more extensive than his. She thought he would undoubtedly find it a struggle.

Thomas noticed the eyes. "Hey, we didn't just talk about writing, we talked about quite a few things, actually."

"Like what?" asked Jody curiously.

"You know, police stuff, SOGGIE stuff. The good old days."

"Hmm, yeah. Back when you were lean and fit," Jody joked.

"Hey, I'm still okay. You should see Johnno now. He's really let himself go." Thomas smiled inside, pleased with his abilities to be such a natural liar. The words just flowed out, he barely had to even think about it. *Fuck*, he thought, *I'm that good I even convince myself I'm telling the truth.*

"Yes honey, you are. I'm a very lucky woman to have a husband that looks like you do. All the girls at tennis are jealous of me."

Thomas paused for a moment to think how many of the girls at tennis he had actually slept with. He couldn't remember.

"Thank you. You're still a MILF yourself," he said, cheekily to his wife. He liked talking like that to her. In the beginning they spoke in bedroom tongue all the time, but now he couldn't remember the last time they had spoken dirty with each other.

"Thomas!" she exclaimed, blushing.

"What? Take it as a compliment."

Jody pulled out a pre-packaged Asian stir-fry sauce. "Alda and Xavier are in the living room. Can you keep an eye on them please? I'm going to start prepping dinner then I need to go fill in the Census. It's Census night tonight."

"Fuck the Census!" exclaimed Thomas.

"Excuse me? Watch your language, the children are just in there!" Jody pointed to the living room where the TV set was blasting away with the song *Let It Go*. Thomas couldn't believe the pair were watching the movie *Frozen* again.

What is up with him? thought Jody. *His choice of words lately has been deplorable.*

Thomas was unapologetic. He continued, "You shouldn't even waste your time filling the thing out. I don't want our personal information going to the government. All it is, is just another way for them to Big Brother us. I hate that shit."

"Well, that's pretty weird coming from someone who worked for the government for so long. The government paid our bills!"

"Yeah, well I only worked for the State Government and they were bad enough. Fucking wanting to know what colour undies you had on each day!"

"Thomas! Shh," his wife was pointing to the living room again. Thomas thought there was no way the children could hear him over Elsa's vocals.

"I really have no idea why you're so against it," his wife retorted. "They use the data to help plan infrastructure. You know, plan for the future?"

"Whatever, Jody, do what you like." Thomas headed to the fridge and grabbed out a beer. He then walked out of the kitchen, leaving Jody slightly dumbfounded. *Since when had her husband had such a dislike for the government?* She asked herself. She had never heard him carrying on like this before. He had loved being in VICPOL.

Jody found Thomas sitting on the back deck gazing into nowhere, drinking the beer. She had seen him grab the drink out of the fridge and wondered how it had suddenly appeared in there. She thought she'd better smooth things over. She didn't want the kids to see them fighting, or not speaking with each other, which in her mind was much worse.

She pulled up one of the other seats on the deck so she was

close to her husband. "Honey, if you don't want me to fill it in then I won't, okay?"

Thomas looked at her and smiled. He suddenly remembered why he'd married her. She really was a good woman and she respected his opinion.

Jody had a slightly concerned look on her face. "Um, we won't get in trouble, will we? I mean, for not completing it?"

Thomas laughed and said, "No, honey. They don't know if a household has completed it or not. Anyway, as I always say, what they don't know won't hurt them."

Jody stared at her husband and thought, *Actually, I've never heard you say that.*

CHAPTER 29

Outer Eastern Suburbs, Melbourne, Victoria

"SO CHERYL MOST CERTAINLY said your appointment is at 0900hrs?" Bianca asked Thomas, who had just turned up at her apartment. She wondered what he had told Jody about having to go to work so early. She then dismissed the thought, as it wasn't her problem.

"Yes. Here - take a look yourself." He pushed the mobile phone towards her.

"No, no, I believe you. It's just that we have to make sure she's at The Agency then. We only get one shot at this," Bianca stated, as if Thomas didn't already know that.

"She'll be there. You know her, if she tells you to come in she will be there, and David too. That's pretty much a given."

"She'll get a surprise when you're not there on time," said Bianca, thinking how she was never late for one of her scheduled Agency appointments.

"No, well, I was actually often late. I think she will get more of a surprise when the place is blown to smithereens!" Thomas laughed. Bianca was enjoying the man's Carlin-esque side that had recently reared its head.

Bianca stopped laughing at the dark humour and said: "Thomas, the coffee shop just around the corner from here is open now. It's just past 6.00 am. It opens early weekdays. Do you mind going and getting me a coffee, please? Here's my swipe key." She fluttered her brown eyes at him.

"Of course, baby. Do you mind checking that everything is squared away ready to go, please?"

"Absolutely, Thomas. I'll do a check while you are out."

Thomas patted his pants pocket to make sure he had his wallet and headed out of the bedroom. As he was walking away Bianca suddenly called out to him.

"Hey, Thomas."

He stopped and turned around. "Yeah, what's up?"

"I just wanted to say thank you."

Thomas looked at her lovingly at this rare moment of affection from her. However, he couldn't help asking, "Why's that, baby?"

"Because you have helped me open my eyes," she answered, immediately returning to rummaging through the handbag on her lap.

Thomas smiled at her and walked off. *Women,* he thought, *they rarely make sense.*

Thomas entered the bedroom holding two takeaway coffees. Bianca was on one of her mobile phones.

"*Ci vediamo presto. Ciao bella,*" Bianca said down the line.

He didn't know what it meant and once again kicked himself for being such a typically ignorant Australian.

Bianca ended the call, locked her screen and looked up. She was surprised to see Thomas standing there with their coffees. He had been quicker than she had calculated. *Typical,* she thought, *when you are in a rush it's like they're preparing your wedding cake, but today, just when I'm wanting some time, the barista behaves in a manner befitting his favourite comic book character.*

"Who was that?" Thomas enquired as he handed Bianca her cup.

"Thanks. It was just my mum, her weekly welfare call. She was making sure I was still alive." Bianca took a sip of her coffee and put it down on the floor.

"Ha, yeah parents, they never stop treating you like a kid."

The pair shared a smile and Bianca pulled out the covert body armour that she had stored under her bed. She slipped the combined knife and ballistics vest over her head and pulled it down, securing it around her body.

Thomas stopped smiling. "Where did you get that? That's not Agency issue."

"The Agency doesn't issue vests," said Bianca, wondering what Thomas was on about. "Where do you think?" She asked as she pulled her black t-shirt over the top of the armour.

It didn't take long for Thomas to answer. "Well, I'm guessing the farm."

"You would be guessing correct. A gift from my uncle."

"I didn't see him give you that."

"I got it ages ago." Bianca put on her favourite wool sweater. It was a warm cable knit and sat neatly over the top of her vest and t-shirt.

Thomas shook his head. "You worry way too much."

"And you don't worry enough," Bianca said as she picked up her coffee from the floor and took a sip.

"Hey," he retaliated. "I have a vest. I'm not a complete idiot, you know. It's an over-body style, courtesy of VICPOL. It's way too bulky to put on now. I'll put it on later. Plus, I'd look like a suicide bomber walking out of this apartment building with it on. Just the type of attention we want to draw to ourselves today, huh?"

"Fair enough, each to their own," Bianca replied as she struggled to pull on her tight boots. She wondered why she had paid nine hundred dollars for them when the things were almost impossible to get on. Finally the leather succumbed to her strength.

"Well, I think I'm ready. Now or never, hey?"

"That's right. We have to do this, we made a promise we would end this fucked-up situation we've somehow found ourselves in. It does, however, give me something to actually write about now!" Thomas was almost laughing. Bianca wasn't sure if it was because of nerves or because the man actually thought he was amusing.

"Is the car packed up?" he asked Bianca as he took a sip of his own sugared coffee.

"Yep, I've done a check and everything is squared away," she answered, thinking Thomas should already have known she would have checked a thousand times just to make sure. Thomas's eyes suddenly scanned the room. He noticed something had been missing since he'd arrived.

"Hey, where did you say Samson was again?"

"He's staying with a friend."

"I didn't think you had any real friends."

"I never said that."

"Yes you did."

Typical man, thought Bianca, *never really listening.* "No, what I said was that I don't particularly trust people with him. But I will say that yes, I don't particularly have that many friends. In all honesty, I actually don't like that many people. They are generally a pain in the backside."

A smile crept across Thomas's face as he remembered how he hadn't appeared to have been a pain in her backside the other day in her aunt's bathroom. *Quite the opposite actually*, he couldn't help but think.

Bianca noticed the stupid grin on Thomas's face. "Why are you looking so happy?"

"Because I'm with you."

Bianca smiled back at Thomas. She thought once more that he really could be a sweetheart. He continued, "And because we are going to blow the shit out of The Agency."

Bianca laughed her nervous laugh. Thomas noticed that it sounded more nervous than usual.

"Are you nervous, baby?"

"I rarely get nervous, Thomas, but yes I am a little. I mean we are taking extreme measures here. People are going to die." Bianca took another sip of her coffee, avoiding eye contact.

"Yes. Cheryl is going to die, and David, and probably whoever else is in the building." Thomas seemed indifferent about it.

"But what if we're wrong? We really have no evidence yet, I mean not strong evidence."

"Bianca, Cheryl is an absolute nutter and definitely knows what's going on with The Agency. We know for a fact that they have us studying each other. Why? I don't know, and to be honest I've come to the conclusion that I actually don't care. All I know is that I will not be someone's subject and I know you feel the same, you said it yourself."

"I do, I do. I mean this was actually my plan, remember? Remember how you suggested we just go in there and shoot them in the head. Yeah, good plan until your old black pyjama mates show up."

"Well, I didn't know then about your *la famiglia*, did I? I didn't know who they were."

Thomas had googled the Italian word and learnt it meant The Family. He then realised why it was familiar to him, having heard it used in Hollywood movies, many a time.

Bianca raised her eyebrows at him. She hadn't said anything to him about the family. He had worked it out himself. The man was smarter than she had given him credit for.

"Yeah, don't be so surprised Bianca. What, did you think I wouldn't make the connection? I mean come on, who fucking has a fully stocked armoury like that? And I didn't believe for a second he'd obtained them all legally as he told me."

Bianca gazed into Thomas's eyes. They were the most intense colour she had seen them.

"Do you still love me?" she asked as a big grin spread across her face.

"More than you will ever know, baby," Thomas replied thinking of the extra layer of spice this now added to the onion of a woman. He then had to hold his laughter inside himself as he realised he had compared her to the character *Shrek*. That was one movie he had been exposed to more than enough times thanks to his children.

"I believe that may be the truth," she said, and picking up her large tote bag and leather jacket. "Come on, we need to go. We need to get to the location and get set up ready."

CHAPTER 30

Somewhere in Melbourne, Victoria

T HE PAIR ARRIVED ON site earlier than expected. The traffic had been light, and although it was blistery cold, there was no rain.

Utilising satellite imaging, they had pinpointed the most suitable location to take the shot to ensure an accurate outcome. It was 1.8 kilometres from the target, and allowed plenty of time for them to pack up and leave before the emergency services even arrived at The Agency's building to try and work out what the fuck had just happened. Thomas and Bianca had discussed how at first the authorities would be sure to think the building had been subject to some type of internal explosion such as a possible gas leak. Then of course they would jump straight to the sensational conclusion of an ISIS-backed terrorism attack. No way in the world would they initially consider that someone had fired a 50 calibre HE bullet from 1.8 kilometres away, especially with no terrorism motive.

In silence, Thomas and Bianca walked from the vehicle towards their position to set up the weapon when Thomas suddenly spoke. "You know, just out of interest what happened to your attackers? I mean the guy's that raped you?"

To Thomas's surprise, she answered without hesitation. "They got what was coming to them." Bianca paused then continued, "And some still have it coming to them."

Thomas was still registering the answer when Bianca suddenly changed the conversation's tangent. "Thomas, how long before I can see you once this is over?"

Thomas was now seated on the ground setting up the bipod for the rifle to sit on. He looked up at Bianca. Immediately she read his face.

"Baby, unfortunately it won't be for a long time. I mean, I can't stay in Melbourne, that's for sure; and possibly not even Australia. I've already applied for a fly-in fly-out position in a mine in Indonesia, leading their emergency response team."

Bianca wasn't sure what to say so she decided not to say anything. Her Nonna had always said: "God gave you two ears and one mouth to be used in that proportion."

Thomas heard Bianca's footsteps as she started walking away from where he was seated on the ground.

"What you doing, babe?" he called out to his lover.

Bianca replied, "I'm just going back to the car, I left my jacket inside and I'm cold."

Thomas was surprised she didn't already have it on, as it must have been only ten degrees and she seemed to live in that leather jacket.

Bianca opened up the door of Thomas's Range Rover. She reached into her tote bag and pulled out her loaded Beretta 92 pistol. She looked over to where Thomas was. She observed that he was around twenty meters away with his head down, still fiddling away with the McMillan Tac-50. Bianca put her hand back into her bag and pulled out one of her uncle's gifts to her. She attached the gift to her namesake as she approached Thomas.

"Hey Thomas, you know what?" Bianca asked as Thomas sat on the ground concentrating hard on calculating some of the bullet ballistics required to make an accurate shot at such a distance.

"What, baby?" he asked, without even bothering to look up.

"You really don't worry enough," and with that Bianca emptied three rounds from her silenced Beretta into Thomas's chest.

Bianca stood there like a statue as Thomas's body awkwardly slumped to the ground. She thought she should probably walk up to him and put a bullet in his head just to make sure, but she'd been told a few shots in the chest would suffice, and anyway she didn't want to get blood splatter on her leather jacket or designer jeans. She suddenly flashed back to her childhood and the moment when she had seen the blood splatter across her father's face. The little girl had watched on in secrecy as her father and uncle slit some unknown's throat. Unbeknownst to Bianca, this was a defining moment for her.

Bianca immediately turned her back on her subject. She pulled her phone out of the pocket of her skinny jeans and sent a text: *My appointment is complete.* Bianca patted her head to make sure her hair was still tucked up in the hat she'd put on before they left. She glanced over at Thomas's old VICPOL ballistics vest that lay on the ground near the Tac-50 weapon case and shook her head, thinking back to Thomas's earlier comment about the piece of armour.

Bianca walked back to Thomas's vehicle and grabbed her tote bag from inside. She placed it on her shoulder and started to walk away from the scene without looking back. She was surprised at her utter lack of emotion. She felt indifferent, but she couldn't help thinking how much she would miss the sex and his pretty face. *Shame,* she suddenly thought, *the man really knew how to fuck.*

Suddenly two black Toyota Prados arrived at the scene.

"Bianca, get in."

The door was already held open for her and she ran to the car and took a seat next to her boss. She immediately turned her head and looked out the window at the scene she had created. Three men in what looked like biological suits scurried over towards Thomas's body from the other Prado. She turned her head away. She had seen enough.

"You okay?" Cheryl asked as the car she and Bianca were in started to drive away from the scene.

"As usual, I'm just fine. Dumb ass didn't even wear a vest."

Cheryl looked at her subject and smiled, "You are such a bitch, Bianca." She paused and looked her subject straight in the eye. "And that's why we love you." Cheryl put her hand on Bianca's knee and started rubbing it lightly. She continued,

"Do you remember what I said to you at the start - 'Hell hath no fury like a woman scorned?' I truly believe you are capable of anything."

The women looked at each other and laughed.

Bianca stopped laughing. *That is right, Cheryl,* she thought. *I am capable of anything.*

Blessed are the peacemakers

Matthew 5:9

Somewhere in Melbourne, Victoria

"STINGS LIKE ALL BUGGERY. Fuck going through that again."
"You really took one for the team. Welcome officially to The Department."

"Thanks ... I think," Thomas managed to say, groaning in pain.

"Here mate, suck on this. It'll help ease the pain until we get you some of the really good shit." David handed Thomas an instant pain reliever known as a 'Green Whistle'.

"Just take the fucking thing off me," Thomas said in agony.

"Just about to do that. We need to inspect the damage."

"Bitch. The bitch actually shot me. I can't believe she actually did it."

"Well Christo, Cheryl did tell you she would."

"Yeah, but I still didn't think she'd actually go through with it. And she fucking shot me three times!"

"You're lucky she didn't shoot you in the head. She probably would have if Cheryl hadn't told her to take centre of mass shot at around twenty metres. Stay still while we get this vest off you," David said as he cut off Thomas's sweater and removed the concealed ballistics vest.

"Mother fucker," Thomas said in pain between sucks of the whistle.

"Yep, your chest's a mess, but nothing you'll die from. Bruises will be there for a bit, mate. Hope you've got a good story for your wife." David laughed.

Thomas felt like punching him. He probably would have, except he could barely move let alone raise his arm.

"Come on mate, we need to get you to the car and back to The Agency to clean you up and sort you out. Cheryl said you're to have a few weeks off to recover before we assign you your new role within The Department."

"Looking forward to it," Thomas managed to spit out in between the groans as the men got him onto his feet, assisting him into the back seat of the Prado.

"What? The time out or your new role with The Department?" David asked with interest.

"Both."

Bianca sat silently in the backseat of the 4WD, staring out the window. Flashes of buildings and traffic went by. Everything was a blur and she found herself lost in her own thoughts. She thought of all the people inside those buildings and driving those cars, and wondered what they were doing and what they were thinking. She pondered on what part they played in the bigger scheme of things. Were they important to anyone at all?

Cheryl had stopped rubbing Bianca's leg and was now on her phone texting someone. Bianca realised her boss must have decided she had consoled her enough.

"You know I need the 50 Cal back, don't you?" Bianca said suddenly, coming out of her trance-like state.

Cheryl looked up from her phone. "Sorry, what was that?"

"The 50 Cal, I need it back. As I told you, it was only on loan."

"Yes, yes of course. The boys will pack it up and drop it back to you sometime soon. You know, you never did tell me how you got your hands on that." Bianca couldn't help but notice Cheryl's look of inquisition.

"What does it matter anyway?" asked Bianca still unsure if Cheryl actually knew anything about her family or not. She thought she well may, given Cheryl's background and The Department's ability to obtain information. Bianca would have been surprised if they hadn't made any connections. Nevertheless, she had never mentioned anything about her family's background - and she wasn't about to start. Especially if it had been an oversight by The Department. The family protected each other.

Cheryl looked at her and smiled. "You're right, it doesn't matter. It served its purpose and I'm so glad you were able to work it into the plan to take out Thomas. You're a real thinker, Bianca. I couldn't be more excited to have you on the inside of The Department now. I have an interesting job lined up for you. I think you'll be pleasantly surprised." Cheryl started to rub Bianca's thigh again, affectionately running her fingers lightly from her knee all the way up to the inside of her legs.

Bianca smiled back at her boss. "Sounds intriguing, what's the job?"

"Not now, hun. We're going to get you back to your apartment. Let you have a little bit of R and R before I get you to come back to work and onto your first official Departmental job within the Agency project."

"Will Samson be there?" Bianca asked, remembering she had given the cat to Cheryl to look after, in case the plan had gone to shit and she ended up with a bullet in her head.

"David will drop him off a bit later, and he'll have a special gift for you as well."

A smile spread across Bianca's face as she thought about seeing her precious pet. "What's the gift? Is it a pair of diamond stud earrings?" She laughed, but secretly thought she wouldn't mind a pair.

Cheryl was impressed with Bianca's line of thinking. She had just shot someone and all she was worried about was her pet. *No wonder I can't help but be attracted to her*, she thought. *She's a lot like myself, just not with my facial bone structure or level of intelligence.*

"No, it's a bottle of wine," Cheryl replied.

"Even better."

Cheryl smiled inwardly and returned to her phone, texting away as fast as a Japanese schoolgirl. *I know that woman better than she knows herself*, she thought as she tapped away. She suddenly caught her thoughts and stopped the texting.

There is something I don't know about her... but I will.

Cheryl returned to texting. The end of the text read: *'Plan executed perfectly. Full report tomorrow'*. She hit the send button. She glanced over at Bianca, who was staring out the window again. Cheryl wondered if she was thinking about anything other than her beloved Samson or drinking a glass of wine. *Maybe she was thinking about Thomas? Maybe she was questioning her own actions?*

"What you thinking?" Cheryl asked in a loving, almost motherly manner.

Bianca turned to face Cheryl's perfectly formed face. "Oh, nothing important, nothing important at all."

"That's good to hear. We wouldn't want you to mess up that pretty head of yours with overthinking things now, would we?"

"No chance of that. It is what it is."

"It certainly is," Cheryl replied, then leant in and softly kissed Bianca's lips.

Bianca pulled away, thinking of the driver, with whom she wasn't familiar. Cheryl read her actions.

"Oh, don't worry about him, he knows his place. Now let's get you back to your apartment before David turns up. I have something else special for you."

Bianca smiled and blushed at the same time. She had always liked anything with the word 'special' associated with it.

CHAPTER 32

Somewhere in North East Victoria

"HERE YOU GO, *Zio*," said Bianca, handing her uncle the weapon case that housed the McMillan Tac-50 calibre rifle.

Tony smiled and took the case from his niece, pulling her in with one arm and giving her a kiss on either cheek. "How did she go?" he asked, referring to the weapons system.

"It served its purpose," Bianca answered.

"Well I didn't hear anything on the news. Since you had wanted the HE bullet, I was kinda expecting you might be blowing something to pieces." Tony looked at Bianca curiously.

"All rounds are still there, *Zio*," Bianca said with a smile.

Tony shook his head. "You really are a calculated creature aren't you, Bianca? A real Beretta. It's a shame your father wouldn't let you join the business; you would have performed well and made him really proud." Tony paused for a moment, looking a little despondent. "Yes, if only he could see you now," he sighed, "So beautiful, so independent..." Tony looked around, realising Bianca was missing something and also that she wasn't completely independent. "Where's Samson?"

"He's still in my car - I need to go get him."

"And Thomas?" Tony asked with a bushy eyebrow raised.

"That one's done and dusted," Bianca answered as she started to make her way back to her dirt-covered Volkswagen, thinking it too needed a good dusting.

Tony looked bemused. "Thought as much. Margaret will be upset. She really liked him."

"Yeah, well didn't we all?" Bianca replied thoughtfully as she made her way back to her vehicle.

"Tony? Bianca? You guys coming in?" Margaret called out from the front veranda of the farmhouse.

"Hi Margaret. Yes, I'm just getting Samson," Bianca called in reply as she pulled the cat cage from her front passenger seat.

"Okay, dinner's almost ready," Margaret yelled back.

Bianca looked at her watch. It wasn't even five-thirty yet. Bianca had timed the trip so she arrived at the farm just before dusk. Any later than that and most assuredly her Volkswagen would have an encounter of the not-so-friendly kind with a kangaroo. She thought her uncle and aunt were really starting to show their age.

"Tell Margaret I'll be there in a tick. I need to get this put back to where it belongs," said Tony, patting the weapon case lightly as if it were a well-behaved small child.

Bianca nodded and started walking towards the farmhouse, carrying Samson in his cage. The sounds of the horses and the babbling of the brook felt comforting to her. She felt as if she was home, even though this wasn't her home. Samson started to meow.

"Yes, baby, Mummy will let you out in a moment," Bianca said to her pet, thinking that if she let him out in the yard with the chooks Margaret would lose her shit.

"Bianca, so good to see you again, and so soon!" declared Margaret as she hugged and kissed her niece. The aunt pulled away and looked Bianca up and down. "You really look beautiful. Have you put on weight?" Margaret immediately realised what she had said and backtracked. "I'm sorry, that didn't come out right. It's just you were so skinny when you were here last, and you look a little *healthier* now." Margaret lowered her head as she thought back to 'The Rule of Holes' – *When you are in one, stop digging.*

Bianca noticed how uncomfortable Margaret was, and decided to put her out of her misery. "It's okay, Margaret. I have put on a kilo...or two." Bianca had noticed in the past week that her skinny jeans were even tighter than usual. She thought her age must finally be starting to catch up with her appearance.

"Well you look great," Margaret replied, happy at Bianca's response.

"Thank you," said Bianca, just to be polite. She wasn't at all happy that her sudden weight gain was noticeable. She would have to slog herself on the rowing machine, as she was due back at The Agency the following week to start her new role within The Department. *Cheryl will have absolute kittens if she thinks I'm getting fat,* Bianca thought to herself.

Bianca put Samson's cage on the living-room floor. She squatted down and let him out. He started to wander around the room as if he owned the joint. Bianca liked the way the cat asserted its authority without having to say a word. She wished Samson was a man - he would be perfect for her.

"Can I give Samson some milk, please?" Bianca asked politely, opening the refrigerator.

"Of course you can. There's a couple of cartons in there. Just use the one with the oldest date. We need to use it up before it goes off."

Bianca got out the almost sour milk from the fridge door and poured some into a little dish for her beloved feline. Samson was wrapping himself between her boot-clad legs. He knew what was coming his way. She bent down and put the dish on the floor, and immediately Samson started to lap it up. Just then Tony walked through the front door.

"The stew smells great. Lamb, right?"

"Yes darling, it's lamb. Where have you been?"

Tony looked at Bianca. Bianca realised she had forgotten to mention that Tony had to put something away.

"Oh sorry Margaret, I was meant to tell you that Tony had to go do something. Me and my goldfish memory," Bianca laughed nervously.

Tony and Margaret joined in her laughter. "It's okay, *cara*, you've obviously had a lot on your mind lately," said Tony, thinking what Bianca had been up to without really knowing exactly what she had been up to.

"Actually, no. Haven't had much on my mind at all. Just been doing some art," replied Bianca truthfully. The combination of her uncanny ability to emotionally shut off, consume alcohol and get lost in a painting meant that Bianca really hadn't thought much about what had gone down in the past few weeks.

"Here Bianca, a little something for you," Tony said as he placed a small clear plastic bag containing white powder into Bianca's hand.

Bianca immediately put the little bag into the back pocket of her jeans. She smiled. "Thanks *Zio*. You are *so* good to me."

"How's Thomas?" Margaret asked innocently, pretending that she hadn't seen the gift giving.

Tony shot his wife a look from across the kitchen. Margaret read it straight away and her forehead creased.

"Unfortunately, that relationship was doomed from the start," Bianca stated in her matter-of-fact manner.

"Oh, that's a shame. I thought he was really taken with you. It's a very long time since I actually saw a man look at a woman the way he looked at you."

Bianca suddenly became interested in the conversation. "How do you mean, Margaret?"

Margaret stood over the stove and started to heap huge servings of her lamb stew into bowls. "What I mean is, he looked at you with complete love in his eyes. And yes, I said love, not just lust."

Bianca had a flashback. She could see Thomas's blue eyes looking deeply into hers, and suddenly felt like being sick.

"I wouldn't go that far," Bianca managed to say between her sudden shallow breaths.

"Oh my dear, but I would," Margaret replied, without turning around from the stove.

Bianca suddenly ran off towards the bathroom. She made it to the toilet in time not to make a mess all over the bathroom floor.

Tony and Margaret could hear her vomiting. After a couple of minutes Margaret instructed her husband: "You better go check on her. Make sure she's okay. Maybe she has a bug?"

Tony started to make his way out of the kitchen when Margaret couldn't help but put her two cents in: "You know, Tony, I don't like you giving her that stuff. It's not good for her."

Tony ignored his wife and made his way down the hall towards the bathroom. "Bianca? *Cara?* You okay?" he called out cautiously as he approached the bathroom door. The door was partially open and he found Bianca sitting on the blue tiles of the bathroom floor. She was wiping her mouth with a towel.

Bianca looked up and managed a smile. "I'm fine, *Zio*. Well, if you get me a *vino* then I'll be fine."

Tony smiled back. "*Certamente*, anything for you." He left Bianca to clean herself up and made his way back into the kitchen.

Margaret stopped slicing the crusty bread. "Is she okay? Does she still want dinner?"

Tony grabbed a wineglass from a kitchen cupboard and started to pour a glass of red wine as he answered his wife: "As always, she is just fine."

• CHAPTER 33 •

Somewhere in Canberra, Australian Capital Territory

"WHERE'S DAVID?" MICHAEL ASKED Cheryl as she walked into his office.

"I'm sorry, didn't I tell you? He couldn't make it. He had some urgent findings to collate. Subject 006, Brad Saunders, took a turn yesterday. It appears his PTSD was worse than we thought," Cheryl said, admiring the new red shellac on her fingernails.

"What? A turn? When were you going to tell me?" said Michael, exasperated at the woman.

"It only happened yesterday. A full report is coming your way; however, it's not looking good. I think he'll be of no use for the project any more. He's too far gone. David is working on the report now."

"Okay, okay. Fair enough. *I'll* make that call after going over the report. Now, I received the latest report regarding the happenings between Subjects 003 and 008. Very interesting, very interesting indeed," Michael said, stroking his chin like a stereotypical villain. "However, we need to have a talk about what happens next. As you know, given the outcome, and a lot of arse licking from me, the Minister has decided not to completely abandon the Agency project. However, in saying this, we need to tread carefully and make sure this project keeps moving forward in the right direction..."

"The right direction?" Cheryl asked, looking around the office for a water jug as she had forgotten to bring in her water bottle.

"Yes, that's what I said. You know, we need to keep in mind the overall objective of the project. That is, to show the government how we can use people like her to become who we want them to be. We always need to prove how they're particularly susceptible to proving self-worth, being moulded and trained, and of course then becoming whoever we want them to be. It will make for a whole new generation of citizens. She will be the catalyst."

"Yes, I understand that. I fully comprehend the objective."

"Sit down, Cheryl. You want a coffee?"

"Thank you," she said, taking a seat. "No, just a glass of water will be fine."

Michael walked over to his office door and opened it. He called out to his PA. Before she knew it Cheryl had a glass of water served to her by a blonde wearing a low-cut blouse with cleavage on show. Cheryl could understand why Michael had hired the girl.

"Michael, we may have a problem."

"A problem?" Michael asked, taking a sip of the coffee his PA had given him. By the way she had smiled at Michael, Cheryl thought that was not all the young PA had given him.

"Bianca's family. The Berettas."

"What about them?" Michael asked, looking at his gold watch. He wondered what Cheryl was on about.

"Well I hate to say it, but when The Department highlighted her as a possible subject they may have made a slight oversight..."

"Slight oversight? No need to play your games, Cheryl. Just spit it out."

"Well - and I only just recently found this out through subject 008 - but Bianca's family is Australian Mafia."

"What?" Michael involuntarily spat out some of his coffee.

"I know, I know. No one saw it. I mean, yes she has an Italian name, but so does half of fucking Melbourne. It wasn't until she took Thomas to the farm that it all came together."

"Fuck me, Cheryl, are you sure?"

"Yes, well it does require further intel. We need to see how deeply involved her family is ... and what threat they are, if any at all. I'll put Thomas onto it. I'm going to reveal to Bianca that Thomas is alive and get them onto a new job together. Really, though, he'll be gathering info on the Berettas."

"No you are not!" Michael stated firmly.

Cheryl looked at her boss in surprise. She wondered if he knew something she didn't know.

"Cheryl, I want you to keep those two separated. As part of

the overall objective, we now need to keep studying Bianca and really follow her actions and responses after what she has just experienced. If you let her know Thomas is alive and 'working' for The Department too, it will screw it all up. Remember: overall objective."

Cheryl looked displeased. She took another sip of water and answered: "But what about Bianca's family?"

"Well really, Cheryl, you should be able to obtain that information yourself, shouldn't you? Especially given your relationship with her."

Cheryl glared at her boss. He was sitting back in his leather chair looking pleased with himself when he spoke again. "That's right, I know more than you think I know."

"There is no relationship with Subject 003. Just a mutual understanding. Plus, she wouldn't tell me shit. I trained her well."

"Well, she managed to reveal enough info for subject 008 to put two and two together," Michael said in a way that annoyed Cheryl. He continued: "And those are your words, not mine."

Cheryl was pissed off and slightly embarrassed. But she knew she needed to not show any more emotion. Despite the Botox, she was aware that there still could be tell-tale signs on her face and in her voice. She also knew Michael was holding back on her; that was evident. She would need to proceed with caution.

"You're absolutely correct, Michael. I will obtain the information on Bianca's family. It may not necessarily be obtained by me, but it will be obtained. I will keep Bianca and Thomas separated. They will be assigned completely different jobs for the meanwhile."

"Do what you need to do, Cheryl. As long as Subject 003 is still studied, I'll be happy. Her findings are vital to the project."

"Well, really, she is the project," Cheryl replied, flashing a smile at her boss.

"Very true. You know, I've always had full faith in you, Cheryl. You were an outstanding operator and you really helped with getting this project off the ground. I know it's important to you; however, you need to remember it's not just *your* project. It's a Departmental project. It's a government initiative."

"Of course," Cheryl replied, nodding her head in agreement.

"Good, glad to hear it. Thank you for coming in." Michael stood up to show his subordinate that their meeting was over.

Cheryl got the hint and stood up too, picking up her empty water glass from the desk. "So that's it? That was quick," she stated, thinking how much taxpayers' money had been spent on her flights to Canberra and other expenses just for a fifteen-minute meeting.

"Yes, well I have other business to attend to," said Michael, looking at the luxury watch on his wrist.

"Naturally you do," Cheryl replied as she walked out of the office. She couldn't help but feel that maybe The Agency project wasn't as important to Michael as it was to her. She also felt uneasy at the fact that she knew Michael was withholding information from her. It passed her mind that The Department may have known about the Beretta's the whole time.

Cheryl walked to the PA's desk, stopped in front of it and

placed the empty water glass on it. The young girl looked up from her typing, glanced at the empty glass and then at Cheryl.

"Don't worry, honey, I didn't suck him completely dry," Cheryl couldn't help but say as she proceeded to walk to the lift lobby. She had a little laugh to herself.

The PA looked as if she was about to die, and for a moment she secretly hoped she would.

CHAPTER 34

South Melbourne, Victoria

"MY GOD, WOMAN, YOU'VE got fat on me!" exclaimed Cheryl, looking at Bianca in disgust.

"I've put on like two kilos, Cheryl."

"Hmph, is this what happens when I give you a couple of weeks off? You let yourself go?"

"It's okay, it's nothing I can't get rid of," Bianca lied a little, remembering how she had really struggled to get back into her size 6 jeans.

"Yeah, you better. You know I don't employ fatties, nor do I fuck them either."

Bianca hung her head a little. Cheryl noticed and thought she'd better bring Bianca's confidence back up. She needed the woman's head to be in the right space for what was about to go down.

"Since you are now employed internally by The Department, you won't be subjected to any more wellness checks - that's for our subjects only."

"Thank fuck for that," Bianca said just as David entered the room. Bianca ignored him. He took a seat and put his Surface Pro on the desk.

"Have you told Bianca about her probationary period yet?" David piped up from behind the screen of his device.

Bianca's eyes widened. "Probationary period? You've got to be kidding me? Given what I've done, I think I've proven myself ten times over." She looked pissed off.

"Yes, David's right. I completely agree, Bianca, but it's Departmental policy. Rules are rules." Cheryl took a drink of water and continued: "Bianca, take a seat. So, from our previous discussions, you are very clear on the objective of The Agency Project and why the government initiated such a program?"

"Yes, Cheryl. I understand. I'm happy to now be part of it. I mean, on *this* side." Bianca gave Cheryl a knowing look.

"Well, that's very pleasing to hear. We require your utmost confidence and trust. The subjects can't get wind of what is going on. You are the exception, Bianca, but then you have always been exceptional." Cheryl smiled at Bianca in a loving yet manipulative way.

"Thank you," replied Bianca, thinking how nice it was that her boss appreciated her aptness.

"Now, let's chat about your next job ... and once I've briefed you I need you to hang around. I've got a shitload of paperwork for you to fill out."

"And how will I do that?" Thomas asked his boss.

"You'll be partnered with her." Cheryl walked over to the door, opened it and called out, "Bianca, honey, come in here, will you please?"

Bianca walked into the room from the little office where she had been busily completing a whole heap of boring Departmental paperwork. She was wearing her usual attire of leather and denim, except it appeared to Thomas that she had invested in a new pair of designer boots. She looked as if she had seen a ghost.

"No fucking way!" said Thomas, sending Cheryl daggers.

Bianca was silent. David was sitting in a chair watching for her lack of movement or sudden reaction.

Finally Bianca spoke: "Well I have to say, when I woke up this morning I wasn't expecting this!"

"You're not the only one," retorted Thomas, speaking on his own behalf.

The pair looked at Cheryl, who had a big smile on her face as she thought how well her plan was playing out.

Bianca looked back at Thomas. "So you were obviously wearing a vest, then?" she asked, already knowing that she was correct.

"Obviously," Thomas replied in a smug tone.

"How's the bruises?" Bianca asked.

"Almost all gone."

Liar, Bianca thought to herself, knowing full well the damage the shots would have caused even with a ballistics vest on.

Cheryl butted in: "So this obviously begs the question of why I got you two to do what you both did?"

"Yes, well, that did just pass my mind," Bianca said sarcastically.

"Bianca, hun, you know I always only want what is best for you, don't you?"

"Yes Cheryl, I know that."

"Well, I needed both you and Thomas to prove yourselves to us so you could join The Department and keep The Agency project from being shut down. It's a great initiative, and now that you are officially on the inside, you will see that." Cheryl took a sip of water and continued: "The dynamics between you two would be almost impossible to find again and because of this, The Department has now allowed for The Agency project to expand. I have an important job for you both," lied Cheryl.

"I don't want to work with that bitch. She fucking shot me!" Thomas exclaimed, looking straight at Bianca.

"Oh, Thomas. She only did that because I told her to." Cheryl got off her seat and walked over to Bianca. "Isn't that right, hun?" - and with that she gave Bianca a kiss on the lips and Bianca kissed her boss back, wrapping her arms lightly around her waist. She was happy that her minor weight gain obviously wasn't as disgusting to Cheryl as she had made out it was.

Thomas looked on in shock. He wasn't sure what to make of the scene. He was angry, but at the same time turned on seeing the two attractive women making out in front of him. He felt himself unintentionally harden inside his pants. He looked over at David. David had a big smile on his face and Thomas could tell he too was enjoying the moment.

Cheryl stopped kissing and pulled away from Bianca. "Oh, Thomas don't look so surprised. You're not the only one who couldn't help but be taken with her. This time though, try not to be so rough with the girl, and leave some honey for me." Cheryl winked at him.

Thomas noticed Bianca blushing, but he stayed resilient. "There won't be a next time," Thomas said in a firm manner, thinking back to the promise he had made to himself to be faithful to his wife now that Bianca was out of his life. Then he suddenly realised the problem was that Bianca wasn't out of his life. She was back in it with a vengeance.

No, he thought to himself. *Never again. I need to be the man my family thinks I am.*

"Ha, that's what they all say. Take a seat, you two. I have a briefing to give on your new job. Bianca, it's what I briefed you on, and Thomas what I also briefed you on; but let's now go over it together, since you need to work as a team."

Cheryl noticed Bianca looking at David, who was tapping away on his Surface Pro just as he always seemed to be doing. "Oh, if you're wondering why David is in here, it was just in case you both lost your shit with me. He would have spiced you both," Cheryl laughed.

David looked up. He pulled the can of oleoresin capsicum out his pocket to show Thomas and Bianca that their boss was telling the truth.

"Well I'm glad that didn't happen, because that shit is the worst in the world. I think I'd rather be shot again," said Thomas.

A smile crept across Bianca's face and Thomas immediately noticed the look. "Don't even think about it..."

CHAPTER 35

South Melbourne, Victoria

"IT REALLY DOES NEVER cease to surprise me how well those two handle extreme situations. I mean, did you see Bianca? She just adapted to the fact that Thomas was alive, as well as the news you had planned it all, and that now she would be working with him. She barely batted an eyelid. Amazing. These findings are truly astonishing."

"Well, did you really expect anything less from her?" Cheryl asked with an air of certainty. "In saying that, she was a little surprised to see him sitting there; but she trusts me completely. She very quickly realised it was all part of the bigger plan, plus she is just *so* compliant. That's what I love about that woman."

For a moment Cheryl's eyes resembled those of a love-struck teenage girl. Suddenly they returned to normal and she started scrolling her emails.

"What did you think about Subject 008? What did you think about his reaction?" David asked his boss, interested in her answer.

"David, Thomas's reaction was never going to be as intriguing as Bianca's. I mean, she thought he was dead, for crying out loud. Thomas just thought we'd dismissed her from The Agency project." Cheryl smiled inwardly as she thought what a superb performer she still was.

"He was more vocal though, despite the fact that it should have been less of a shock for him given his inside knowledge. I have to say, though, that after you told him about the job and then brought Bianca in, he put on a wonderful performance."

"Well, that's both the difference and the similarity between those two. Thomas always displays more emotion than her; however, they're both amazing actors when required. So much so, it's sometimes a little concerning. You have quite a bit of data to analyse now."

"Yes, Michael will be pleased. I'll work on it this afternoon for it to go to Canberra." David hadn't yet received that pay rise he was hoping for, but he wasn't going to be giving up on it anytime soon.

"Yes, you can work on it today; however, you won't be sending it off to Canberra," Cheryl stated firmly. "Any findings between Subject 003 and Subject 008 are to remain here at The Agency with me for the meantime."

David looked confused and Cheryl could read the look on his face. "David, you need to trust me on this one. I am your boss and you take orders from me. I know what's best for this project."

The look on David's face had grown from confusion into one of concern. He had stopped typing and was staring at his boss intently. He noticed that her body language gave nothing away. He was lucky she wasn't a subject herself, as all her years in the other department had made her one hard book to read. She was definitely a subject he would almost certainly fail.

"Cheryl, I completely understand and respect your position. This is, however, a little concerning to me. What do I give to Michael if he asks about Thomas and Bianca?" David thought how that pay rise was suddenly looking like a hopeless dream. He had dreamt about upgrading his car and buying the latest cutting-edge microscope for his at-home studies. He could see those dreams fading into the distance.

"You make something up," snapped Cheryl, annoyed that David was questioning her instruction.

"Cheryl, I can make up data and findings, but they're not real. I don't understand what the problem is with just presenting the real findings between Thomas and Bianca?"

Now Cheryl was annoyed. This time it was actually evident to David. David suddenly wished he had bitten his tongue. The look on the woman's face frightened him. Aesthetically correct as she was, she was scary as hell when she was mad. Despite his lack of any type of a sex life, he wouldn't touch the woman with a ten-foot pole, especially when she looked like that!

"David, you know how I feel about insubordination, don't you?" Cheryl managed to raise her eyebrow a little more than usual when asking the question. David noticed it and thought she must soon be due for another hit of her favourite toxin.

"Yes. Yes, I do. I will do as instructed."

"That's a good man. You know, David, you are my wingman. I have your back and I expect you to have mine." Cheryl paused then continued, "I mean, why wouldn't you? I still have a great back." She smiled inside, thinking how firm her backside was for her age.

Not as great as Bianca's, David thought. He realised he was lucky for not verbalising that particular comment. That one definitely would have found him with a serious injury.

"So, just to make things clear, Bianca thinks she is now teamed up with Thomas to study a new possible subject. She thinks the objective of the job is to see if the newest candidate will be a suitable subject for The Agency Project. Yes?"

"That's right," Cheryl replied, lying once again to the doctor. "She thinks they are to study Stacey Klein - she's the girl that killed her father as a teenager after years of abuse – to see if she has enough potential to be a good subject for The Agency project."

David nodded his head to show he understood. "And Thomas, well, he's going along with that, but he knows what he really has to do." Cheryl looked down at her shellac manicure. She was happy to see no paint had started to lift.

"The Berettas," David said knowingly.

"The Berettas. That's correct. I can't believe we didn't pick up on that. I mean, the Department should have before highlighting her as a potential subject. Lazy fuckers in Canberra. Obviously someone was not on the ball at all."

"It is slightly concerning; however, I don't believe Bianca actually has much to do with the family. I truly believe they would never take on the Government. I mean, despite their cache, they have nothing. The Government has all the power in the world and they have a few guns - nothing to be concerned about..." David's voice faded into the space of the small office.

Cheryl looked up from her fingernails. "Well, I'm glad you think that, but I need to know more. I'm not happy with just assuming and surmising about such things. You know what they say about assumption, don't you?"

David was pleased he knew the answer. "Yes. Assumption is the mother of all fuck-ups."

"Correct," answered Cheryl, taking a sip of water from the bottle that seemed to be permanently attached to her. David wondered if the bottle actually contained water or some special government-funded fountain of youth. "And on that note – yes, the Government has all the power in the world, but those people have a very special way of just making you disappear. You don't want to just disappear, do you David?"

David pondered on this as he visualised disembowelled body parts being thrown overboard from some boat into the ocean. He shuddered at the visual.

"Most certainly not," he answered with the mental picture still burnt into his mind's eye.

"Well, you'd best just go along with my instructions then, hadn't you? As I stated earlier, you need to trust me with this one. I'm your boss, plus I would never compromise your position. You are much too valuable to the project. Oh, and to *me*." Cheryl fluttered her mascara-covered eyelashes at him.

"Of course I will," replied David, half lying. Cheryl may have thought him stupid at times, but he wasn't as stupid as she liked to think.

Without counsel plans fail, but with many advisers they succeed.
Prov. 15:22

CHAPTER 36

Inner Eastern Suburbs, Melbourne, Victoria

T HOMAS WAS TRYING TO shake the visual of Bianca and Cheryl kissing each other as he was seated in front of his laptop, but he was finding it a real struggle. As much as he tried concentrating on his research, the image of the lesbianism just kept appearing in front of his mind. He was beginning to be annoyed at himself.

"Come on, Christo," he said under his breath, staring at the screen for anything relevant he could find in regards to the Mafia in Australia. The surname 'Beretta' had not yet appeared in any of his searches on the usual platforms. *They certainly do keep a tight lid on their business*, Thomas thought, at the same time thinking it slightly unusual how obvious Bianca had made it to him.

Maybe she thought she might as well let me know about her family 'cause she thought I would be dead soon anyhow. That conclusion seemed to make the most sense to him. He did, however, think that maybe - just maybe - she was actually trying to scare him, to let him know that if he got on the wrong side of her, he got on the wrong side of the family and that would not result in a happy ending.

After two hours in front of the laptop with no real findings, he couldn't stand the continuous hard-on he had endured. He needed to do something about it. Thomas read the time on his Tissot. It was just after 3pm and Jody was on the school and childcare pick-up run. He thought he'd better be quick – but realised that would be easy, given he was that knotted up over the continuous visual flashbacks.

Thomas turned on the shower in the ensuite and stepped naked into the cubicle. He grimaced for a second as the strong pressure of warm water hit his chest. It was still really tender. He couldn't believe that Jody had believed his paint ball story; however, he was a master storyteller and she was his wife, so of course she believed the story.

He was relieving himself when he suddenly heard the kids running through the house. Although the two of them were only about seventy kilograms combined, they sounded like a herd of elephants.

"Xavier, Alda, don't leave your bags in the hallway please. What have I told you about needing to put them away? Go pick them up and put them in your bedroom," Thomas heard his wife say.

Jody looked around and saw that Thomas had been working on his laptop. His seat had not been pushed back in. She approached the desk and pushed the chair back in, and moved the mouse to light up the computer screen. She quickly scrolled the page. *Australian Mafia*, she thought to herself, *he must be doing some novel research, good for him.*

"Thomas, where are you?" Jody called as she walked into the master bedroom from his abandoned workstation.

"I'm in here, honey, you're welcome to join me," Thomas called back cheekily over the sound of the running water.

Jody stood in the bathroom with her hands on her hips. She was wearing a colourful maxi dress with a denim jacket, and Thomas thought she looked particularly pretty that afternoon.

"Really, Thomas? You couldn't wait until tonight?"

"What? I was just having a shower. Aren't I allowed to have a shower now?"

Jody was doing her best to look serious, but Thomas could tell she was trying not to smile. "Honey, I know you were doing more than having a shower. I am your wife, you know."

Thomas smiled and was glad she wasn't completely pissed at him. "Well, as I said, you're welcome to join me. Actually, I would love for you to join me." He looked down at his hardness, hoping it would turn his wife on.

Jody couldn't help but notice how hard he was, but she was still trying to be proper. "What about the kids? I need to get them afternoon tea - they'll be hungry."

"They're always hungry. Leave them for a tick. They're not going to die from starvation, or anything else for that matter, in the next five minutes."

"Only five minutes?" Jody asked as she locked the bathroom

door and took off her denim jacket. Thomas watched as her maxi dress fell to the floor.

Jody stepped into the shower with her husband. She positioned herself in front of Thomas and pushed into him with her husband facing her back.

"Well, given that we haven't done it in the shower for ages, it might be less than five minutes," Thomas replied, grabbing at his wife's breasts from behind.

"If that's the case, I'll take it as a compliment," said Jody in between her sudden heavy breathing.

"You should. It's all about you, honey," Thomas lied.

Five minutes later the couple were done and the kids were hungry. Jody and Thomas entered the living area where their children were of course watching the usual afterschool TV programmes. Thomas had noticed that the school bags were still sitting in the hallway.

"Where have you been, Mummy? I went looking for you and I couldn't find you. We're hungry," said Alda on behalf of herself and little brother.

"Mummy and Daddy were busy," Jody replied, half blushing.

"What were you *doing*?" Alda asked, looking away from the television screen and up at her parents. It was the first time Thomas had noticed her inquisitive nature. *Maybe she might become a cop, like her dad,* he thought.

Jody looked at Thomas for an answer. Thomas had an answer. He thought that just like the big ones, little girls only needed to know what you wanted them to know. "We were doing Mummy and Daddy things. Now, leave that show for a moment and go pick up your school bags like your mother told you to. You shouldn't have to be told twice."

Alda immediately got up to attend to her bag. Xavier was still caught up in *Paw Patrol*. Thomas noticed his non-compliance. "That goes for you too, Xavier; you're big enough now to put away your things. Go get your bag and put it in your bedroom please. After that you can have some afternoon tea."

Xavier managed to pull himself away from the television set. He ran out of the living room and down the hall. Jody made her way into the kitchen to cut up some fruit for the children. Thomas looked at the TV screen and shook his head. *A pack of dogs who are emergency services? Kids will really watch anything.* He wondered if adults were the same, but in regards to books. He secretly hoped they were, thinking of his own novel that seemed to be progressing at the slowest rate.

Thomas made his way back to his laptop and grabbed his phone, which had been on charge via the laptop's USB. He had a message. He read the message and deleted it, locked the screen and placed the device in his jeans pocket. He noticed that his chair had been pushed back in neatly under the desk. He realised he needed to be more careful about leaving his phones lying around, especially when he never knew who was going to message and when.

Jody was still in the kitchen pouring juice into plastic cups when Thomas walked back in. He wrapped his arms around Jody's waist from behind and whispered in her ear, "Thank you for before, honey, you were great."

Jody stopped pouring the juice and turned her head around

and slightly upwards so she could see her husband. "No need to thank me. I'm your wife, I'd do anything for you. You mean the world to me."

"Ditto," Thomas replied, letting go of his wife's waist, thinking how much softer it felt than Bianca's.

Outer Eastern Suburbs, Melbourne, Victoria

B IANCA OPENED UP HER leather wallet and pulled out her VISA debit card. She scraped the card lightly through the small amount of white powder that she had very carefully tipped onto her Caesar stone kitchen counter top. A perfect white line appeared - a little piece of magic. Bianca couldn't wait to get some of the good stuff into her. She knew it was going to be the really good stuff. Her family wouldn't deal in anything but the highest quality.

She opened up a kitchen drawer, moving the contents around in haste, looking for a straw. Unfortunately, she couldn't find one, so between her fingers Bianca tightly rolled up a five dollar note. *It'll do the job*, she thought to herself, pressing one nostril down with her finger, and at the same time snorting up the line of cocaine.

The effects of the drug were almost instant and Bianca felt

at peace with the world. She glanced across the kitchen counter top and smiled at Thomas.

"Here," she said, cutting another line. "Your turn."

Thomas looked at the substance. He had never taken any serious drugs in his life, but he'd always secretly been curious. He had heard that men couldn't perform on cocaine and this was slightly concerning to him; but then he remembered that he wouldn't need to be concerned with that tonight. He took the rolled-up note from Bianca and did the same as she'd done. He wasn't sure what to expect as the narcotic entered his blood stream. He felt thankful that he didn't immediately drop dead, as society had always told him that, "If you take drugs, you most certainly will die."

"That's the first time I've done that," Thomas admitted.

Bianca looked pleased, just as if she was his first fuck. "Well," she replied, "there's plenty more where that came from," thinking of the full bag her uncle had given her.

"You get it from your family?" Thomas questioned.

"That's right. I don't ask for it though, I know better than that. If they have some to spare or if they're feeling particularly generous, I might be given some."

"Lucky girl," Thomas replied, starting to feel the effects and enjoying them.

"Yes I am. I'm also lucky I don't get it given to me too often. It's highly addictive and will fuck you over if you have too much. Then you're no use to anyone."

Thomas nodded his head in agreement. "But a little every now and then is ok?"

"Absolutely."

Bianca walked out of the kitchen, leaving the little bag on the Caesar stone counter top, thinking she might soon be back for some more. She made her way into the living room and turned on her iPod. Jack Johnson starting playing out from the device. She took a seat on the couch and Thomas did the same. He couldn't help but notice Samson staring at him from the armchair. Thomas glared back at his feline nemesis. For a moment he felt as though he was having *déjà vu.*

He came out of it and couldn't hold his tongue. "I have to be honest, Bianca. I don't trust you for a second. You're lucky I'm even here - you fucking shot me!"

Bianca couldn't help but smile. "You're really going to have to get over that. I mean, especially if we're going to be working together. I've moved on from what *you* did."

"What *I* did!" exclaimed Thomas. "I didn't shoot you. Your intentions were to kill me and you didn't give a flying fuck."

Bianca started to look a little more serious. "That's not true. I mean, yes, I did shoot you, but that was only because I felt it was required, given the situation, and of course The Agency's influence. However - and let's be clear on this - I didn't not give a flying fuck. You know how I feel about you, but you also know how I feel about The Agency and now The Department."

Thomas interrupted her: "I know how you feel about Cheryl..."

"Cheryl is a bitch. Plain and simple. However, she is also someone I admire and look up to. She has been like a mother to me."

"Like a mother?" Thomas interrupted. "Well that's highly disturbing, considering you do sexual acts with her. Wrong on every level, Bianca." Thomas shook his head in disapproval.

"Thomas. I said *like* a mother, she's *not* my mother. Thank fuck. Mine's bad enough."

Thomas looked at her seriously, his blue eyes meeting Bianca's big brown eyes. "She uses you. She uses her position of authority and her looks to manipulate you. She plays you."

Bianca stared back into his eyes and said: "Well, that's what The Agency does, isn't it? They use people. Innocent people. People who are most vulnerable. I don't agree with the objective of The Agency at all. The person who came up with the initiative from The Department is completely fucked. The Agency project is what is wrong on every level."

"But here you are working for them and jumping at their every request. You don't make sense at all, Bianca." Once again Thomas shook his head.

"As do you, too; but I know how you felt about being a subject - same as me. I mean, that's why you're here ... amongst other things..." Bianca gave the man one of her sly smiles.

Thomas knew the smile and retaliated with: "I only agreed to come over here so we could sort our shit out," thinking back to his promise. "We're not stupid and I think it was obvious to both of us that we individually only agreed to The Agency's plan so as to get ourselves deeper inside The Department. We just thought we'd be going it alone."

"Yes, yes we did. However, I'm happy I'm not going it alone." She focused her eyes back on him.

"Don't even start that shit with me," Thomas replied, trying to shake off the sudden sexual tension that had entered the small space between them.

Bianca moved in closer to him on the couch. Thomas could smell her scent - a seductress in his nasal passage. "Thomas, I saw the look on your face as you watched Cheryl and me. And I know for a fact that you've fucked her too. You liked watching me with another girl. Actually, you loved it."

Bianca was right, it couldn't be denied. A flush of deep shame came over him as he thought about the afternoon before when he had done his wife hard from behind while visualising it was Bianca. Thomas remained silent and Bianca read his thoughts.

"Come on, come back into the kitchen and have another little line. It will make you feel better." Bianca got up from the couch and held out her hand. Thomas automatically put his hand into hers and allowed her to help him off the couch. The couple walked into the kitchen holding hands like newlyweds. Thomas thought this meeting wasn't going to plan at all; rather, it felt as if it was out of his control. He hated how this always seemed to happen to him, plus the drug was having an obvious effect. He had had the best intentions of just sussing out her agenda in regards to The Agency project, and also to try to gather some more information on her family. Instead he was snorting cocaine and holding the woman's hand. He wished he could just stop thinking with his cock, but it was seemingly an impossible task.

Bianca cut the man a good-sized line and Thomas admired

her from across the kitchen counter. He thought she looked like Aphrodite with a habit, and at the same time he was still in disbelief at his own actions. "I can't believe I'm here doing this with you," were the words that came out of his mouth.

Bianca broke her concentration and looked up at him. "Don't feel bad about it. As a species we are fatally flawed."

This sentence put an inquisitive look on Thomas's face. "How so?" he asked.

"We humans are fundamentally evil..."

"Evil?" Thomas interrupted her. "If we are evil, then what hope do any of us have?"

"You didn't let me finish," said Bianca, undertaking her cutting. "We may be fundamentally evil, but we're saved by grace."

"You mean God's grace?" asked Thomas, thinking how hypocritical Bianca now appeared, speaking about God's grace while cutting lines of cocaine.

"That's the one. Here, these are for you."

Thomas stared down at the kitchen counter top, where little white lines resembled soldiers in drill formation. "You going to have some more?" he asked Bianca, as he snorted up another line like a professional.

"Yes, but not like that."

"Like how then?" Thomas asked her, not at all sure how else to take the drug.

Bianca picked up the little bag and carried it with her into the living room. Thomas followed her. She sat on the couch and pulled up her skirt, revealing her lack of underwear. Finally, she answered: "Well you, Mr Christian, are going to put it up my pussy and lick what you can off her."

He couldn't help but stare at her pink bits, which he swore were winking at him. He carefully emptied a little bit of the powder out onto the coffee table and put his finger in it. He then transferred the substance into Bianca. She moaned with pleasure and relaxed back into the couch.

"You know we'll be up all night doing this now," Bianca said in between her vocals.

"I'm meant to leave some for Cheryl, remember," replied Thomas, thinking back to Cheryl's request at The Agency.

"No, you take it all," another sound escaping from the woman's mouth.

Thomas smiled inside realising how amazing he felt. It was as if he was in some awesome drug-induced dream. His promise to himself seemed a million years ago; and the fact the woman had actually shot him was put aside. It was all about that moment, right then and right there. *Cheryl might think she is the queen bee, but I always get the honey*, he thought to himself as he moved into a comfortable position in preparation for a long night with his head between Bianca's legs.

CHAPTER 38

Outer Eastern Suburbs, Melbourne, Victoria

"I'D BETTER GET HOME - the sun's coming up," Thomas said to Bianca, who had appeared to be in and out of both consciousness and orgasms for the past few hours.

"Yeah, hopefully your old mates don't pull you over for a random MDT. You'll be fucked then," Bianca managed to say before closing her eyes again.

"I certainly hope not," was all Thomas could think to say. As much as he could normally make up a story on the spot, he knew that he would have no explanation for Jody if he got done for drug taking. Jody was completely against drugs. She hadn't even smoked a cigarette in her life. Thomas remembered how she had told him she could never be with a smoker. Not that Thomas had ever smoked. He found smoking a disgusting habit; but coke, well he now had a slightly different opinion on that. That had been anything but disgusting. He hated to admit it, but it had been one of the best experiences of his life.

"My pussy is still aching from you. I've never come so many times in one session, and all from your tongue," Bianca said, sounding slightly alert again.

"Well, my cock is throbbing from not being able to let it out. Wait until I see you next time. I'm going to penetrate you so hard."

Bianca smiled and rested her head back on the couch pillow. "You sure are singing a different tune now. Yesterday you were trying to convince me that you were never going to have sex with me again. Now you can't wait to be inside me - the girl who shot you."

Thomas knew the woman was both shit stirring and testing him a little. He decided not to play her game, accepting that at this point he was no match for her. She had got the upper hand by playing at his weakness, and had only spoken the truth. There was no use denying it. He had an idea of how he would get the upper hand; he just had to wait.

"That's right, baby. You are the girl that shot me, but you are also the girl with the sweetest little pussy. No man in his right mind could resist those lips. Hey, I tried and I failed."

"Epic failure," Bianca couldn't help but respond.

I may have failed in that department, but I'm a success in another department, Thomas thought to himself, referring not just to the multiple orgasms he had given Bianca, but also to some of the other things he had managed to obtain from her in her drugged-up state.

"See you Saturday as discussed," Thomas said as he left Bianca lying on the couch with her skirt still wrapped up around her waist. The clothing item had never managed to make its way completely off her body.

Bianca didn't reply.

Bianca awoke to no headache. *No wonder I love that shit,* she thought to herself. As much as she enjoyed her wine, too much of it still managed to give her a headache that pained like a bitch.

Samson was meowing and sitting at the back door to the little outside terrace area. Bianca got up off the couch, moving her head from side to side, performing her own chiropractic manoeuvres as she straightened her skirt. She opened up the back door for Samson, who dashed straight out to perform his business on his little pet loo mat.

The kettle was put on to boil and Bianca was soon sipping one of her other favourite substances. She walked back into the living room to discover that she and Thomas had gone through three quarters of the bag. It was a fair effort for him, especially given he was a cocaine virgin. She remembered how much he appeared to enjoy it and was surprised by how easily he had taken up the offer. None of her tactics had needed to be deployed; well, except for the *'I'm not wearing any panties'* one - but she couldn't help but deploy that one. It always had mission success... much more reliable than any well-trained army.

Her brew was just what she needed and her head started to clear and retrace the night's events. That was one night she wouldn't be forgetting in a long time.

Bianca made her way into her bedroom and sat on her unslept-in bed with its many cushions still sitting in perfect position. She reached down under the bed to recover her side arm. She felt around with her hand trying to get a grip on the pistol. Unable to locate it, Bianca dropped from the bed onto the floor and looked under the bed.

"Bastard!" she suddenly cried, realising her beloved Beretta was gone. She had left it in its hiding place and now it wasn't there. She raced over to her lingerie drawer just in case she was losing her mind. She thought maybe she had actually left it in its case in that drawer. "Fuck," she said. Her weapons case, silencer and ammunition were also missing.

She immediately made a phone call. Thomas answered. "You know you should message me first before calling," he hissed at her. "You don't know who I could be with or what I'm doing."

"What the fuck, Thomas? Why did you take my sidearm? You had no right. Fucking thief."

Thomas laughed down the phone line. "No right? Well, you did shoot me with it. That might give me a right. Thought I'd best take it off your hands just in case you got the urge again."

"What? Got the urge again? I'm not some trigger-happy psycho, you know? I was only doing as requested. It's Agency issue anyway, not even technically mine for you to take."

Thomas couldn't help but enjoy how pissed off Bianca was sounding. He loved getting some of his own back at her; be it minor, it made him feel good. He wondered why he loved fighting with her and he also wondered why, deep down, she appeared to love it too.

"That's right, baby," he replied. "It is Agency, sorry, Department issue; and that's actually why I took it. The Department asked me to take it off your hands. They said you don't need it any more with the work we're now doing."

Bianca was silent for a moment, computing Thomas's words. She finally spoke. "I'd prefer if you didn't call me baby right at this moment. If that is true, then why didn't Cheryl or David just ask me to hand it in?"

"You liked me calling you baby yesterday, didn't you, baby?" Thomas teased. He continued, "I really don't know. Why don't you just ask them yourself?"

"Oh, don't worry about that, I will." Bianca hung up the phone.

Thomas closed and locked his phone with a little laugh. He loved her when she was angry.

CHAPTER 39

Yarra Valley, Victoria

"AND REMIND ME WHY we're going all the way out here to an archery range?" Bianca asked Thomas, who was driving his Range Rover along the Maroondah Highway.

"Because you agreed to come with me the other night. Plus, I think you'll like it, especially since you now don't have a gun," Thomas commented in what Bianca took as a teasing manner.

"Ha. I'm over that. I spoke with Cheryl and she said you had to hand in your Glock too. Didn't you?"

"Correct. No big deal. Never liked guns anyway."

"Bullshit," Bianca coughed.

"It's true. I can't stand the things. Especially after being shot with one." He looked at Bianca, trying to keep a serious face.

"Oh Thomas, I've heard some doozies in my time, but that by far is the biggest!" She continued: "You get wood just thinking about a weapons system."

Thomas laughed. "Okay, maybe that was a little lie, but I wouldn't go that far. I get wood thinking about something else and that something else just happens to be sitting up next to me." He winked at Bianca.

"Flattery won't get you anywhere, Mr Christian."

"Well, it's certainly worked in the past, Miss Beretta," replied Thomas, thinking back to the response he had received after calling her *Biancaneve* for the first time.

Bianca didn't reply as Thomas pulled off the highway and down a back road that wove through the countryside. A few minutes later they had arrived at the archery range and Bianca helped Thomas carry the archery gear to their spot on the range.

"So the other night you said you've done archery before. However, you don't look too sure what to do." Thomas had noticed that Bianca had just been watching him as he put on his arm guard and finger tab. She continued to observe as he loaded his quiver with arrows, checking the fletchings.

"Um, I've done it like once, at a school camp," Bianca replied, slightly embarrassed.

Thomas noticed her embarrassment and decided to be a nice guy rather than play on it as he would have loved to do. "It's okay, baby, I'll show you."

Bianca allowed Thomas to assist her in setting up ready for the target practice.

"We'll need to adjust the sight on the bow too," he informed her.

"That's enough," Bianca snapped. "I can take it from here. I'm more than capable of shooting a bow and arrow."

Thomas stopped his fussing and picked up his own compound bow from the ground. "As you wish. However, it isn't as easy as it looks." With that Thomas grabbed an arrow from his quiver, armed the bow with it so that the odd colour fletch was sitting outwards. He lined up his sight to the target, drew back the string and released. Bianca watched as the arrow flew through the air and hit the target dead centre. His movements had resembled something out of *Lord of the Rings*.

Bianca grabbed an arrow and clumsily armed the bow; she then tried drawing back the string, but struggled to draw it back to the point where the pulleys locked in. The tension was a lot stronger than she had assumed. Thomas noticed the struggle, but didn't say anything. Inside, he was having a good old laugh. Bianca finally managed to draw back the string in one movement and release. "Fuck me, ow!" Bianca exclaimed, rubbing her left forearm. At the same time the arrow went flying down the range and hit the very outer edge of the target.

A smile crept across Thomas's face. He couldn't hold it in. Bianca noticed it and became pissed off. Pissed off at herself for not automatically being a great archer and also pissed off at Thomas for talking her into doing something that he knew he excelled in. She felt as though it may have been his intention all along to just show off to her.

Thomas rearmed his bow and took another shot. Once again, he displayed deadly accuracy. As annoyed as she was, Bianca couldn't help but be a little impressed. She thought of her idol, Diana the Huntress, who was an exceptional archer. There was something sexy about an archer, that is, if the archer was actually good.

Bianca followed suit, once again struggling with the bow tension. Finally, she pulled back the string in one movement and released. This time she missed the target completely and again let out a profanity as the bowstring had ricocheted off her left forearm once again. Thomas looked at her and said: "Bianca, please put on an arm guard, let me check your sight, and I'll show you a few things."

She decided she'd best give up the stubbornness. Her mother was a stubborn bitch and the last thing Bianca wanted was to become her mother. "Okay, you obviously know what you're doing. Show me."

Thomas got in close to her and repositioned her stance and body. He showed her how to arm the bow in a fluid motion, keep the bow steady and line the sight. Then he assisted her to draw back the bow's string. The couple watched as the arrow did its dance in the air and hit the target in the black section. A big white smiled flashed across Bianca's face. Thomas smiled back at her. At that moment, she was most exquisite creature he had ever laid eyes on.

"Again," she said, still displaying the big smile.

"See, that was much better. A few more goes with me then you can try by yourself."

Bianca nodded her head. She couldn't help feeling the large welt surfacing upon her forearm, but decided not to mention the pain as Thomas coached her on. He was making the point of telling her to bend her left elbow slightly outwards when she released the bow string.

"So how did you become such an expert bow hunter, anyway?" Bianca asked, truly interested in his answer.

"My father was a competition archer. He got me into it as a

child. I don't mean to blow my own trumpet, but as you can see I'm pretty good. I mean, when I was younger I was even better, but then I got damn tennis elbow, so I had to stop. I needed to keep my elbow in order for the police."

"Oh," replied Bianca, who had thought tennis elbow only came from tennis.

"Yeah, well now I just do it every now and then. If I feel it start to niggle, I stop. Same deal with tennis, you know, when Jody and I play couples..." Thomas' sentence faded off as he realised what he had just said.

Bianca pretended not to hear. Instead she fired off an arrow by herself, hitting the black section of the target again.

"Well done!" exclaimed Thomas, proud of his own coaching abilities. "See, with a bit of training, you're a natural! You must get it from your family. I mean, they all have a good eye, don't they?"

Bianca turned her head towards Thomas while keeping her body in the same position. "My family are not archers, but yes they do have a good eye, they love a bit of hunting."

Thomas looked back at her as she took another shot and again hit the target, this time in the blue section. "Yes, well, I guess to be in that business they have to be good hunters. Silent, deadly and leave no tracks, hey?"

Bianca took a good look around the archery range. She observed that there was no one within fifty metres of them. "And what business would that be, Thomas?" she asked, as if she didn't know what he was talking about.

"Baby, come on, you took me to the farm and you told me

yourself. The family business, the drug business. Dealing in narcotics."

Bianca laughed, tipping her head back like a model in a soft drink commercial. Thomas wondered what was so funny and couldn't help asking her, "Why are you laughing?"

"Because narcotics is not the main business. They have other business to keep them busy."

"And what would that be?" asked Thomas, once again floored by Bianca's apparent openness. The Department had portrayed her as usually being like a vault. If this was true, then obviously Thomas held the key.

"Tobacco, Thomas, tobacco."

All of a sudden, it started to rain. The rain fell down on the pair as if God himself was pouring buckets of water on them.

"Fucking Melbourne weather, always spoils your plans," Thomas uttered, looking up into the sky.

"What about my leather jacket?" Bianca commented, concerned how much water it could take before being ruined. She was starting to scramble to pick up the archery gear. Beads of water were streaming down her face and her long hair had a sudden curl.

"No, just leave it," Thomas told her. "We're getting soaked, let's make a dash for it!"

Bianca dropped the equipment she was holding in her hands and put her hand in Thomas's. Together they made a run for it, all the while becoming more soaked. By the time they were back at Thomas's vehicle, they were both wet through to the bone.

Bianca stared at Thomas, thinking how handsome he was with the beads of water running off his hair. She thought she probably just looked like a drowned rat.

Thomas started to laugh, "Well, that came out of nowhere. I'm fucking soaked. I'm going to have to take these clothes off."

Bianca smiled at him as he removed his own leather jacket and shirt underneath, baring his muscular chest. "Well," she replied, "I guess I'll just have to join you then..."

CHAPTER 40

South Melbourne, Victoria

"WHAT'S THAT PERFUME YOU'RE wearing?" Cheryl looked up at Thomas from her typing. "Nice, isn't it?"

Thomas didn't answer. He didn't think it was nice at all. The smell was overpowering in Cheryl's small office and was starting to make Thomas feel ill.

Cheryl continued, "It's Chanel No.5. Classic. Spoiled myself the other day and bought myself a bottle. I haven't owned a bottle of it in years." Cheryl had a happy look on her face, thinking how attractive she must smell.

You should have left it on the shelf, is what Thomas thought. *Chanel No.5. I must remember to put that on my Jody present blacklist.* Most of the items on Jody's present blacklist had been put there by Jody herself. He had locked the items into his cognitive memory. They included vacuums, gardening equipment of any kind; and blenders, unless her *Nutribullet* broke. If that happened, then Thomas was to immediately replace it with a new one. He didn't think Jody would cope by not being able to macerate perfectly good fruit and vegetables into liquid, all because they were apparently so much *healthier* in that form.

Thomas took a sip of water from the glass he had poured himself. He thought it might make him feel a little less nauseated. Cheryl stopped tapping away and spoke: "So Thomas, what information have you for me regarding the Berettas? I'm guessing by your lack of any formal report that you haven't been very successful in that regard?"

"Tobacco." Thomas replied. "They grow and sell tobacco. Illegally of course."

Cheryl looked somewhat interested. "Go on..." she urged.

"The area where one of the Berettas' farms is located formerly had tobacco growing as its main industry. The Berettas came out to Australia sometime in the 1930s during the influx of European immigrants. They were originally based out of Griffith, which by the way is the home of the Italian Mafia in Australia; but Bianca's father and uncle purchased properties in country Victoria. I don't know how many farms or land they actually have control of and how much of it is used to grow the tobacco."

"So they used to grow it legally, but now they don't?"

"Yeah, well, pretty much everyone used to be a tobacco farmer in that area, but now it's illegal. Some years ago, the Government and industry paid them all out. In the past few years, however, the black trade for tobacco has increased something like thirty percent."

"So business is booming for the Berettas?" asked Cheryl.

"So it appears. They ain't short of a quid. They can get their hands on whatever they want - firearms, drugs, you name it. They have their hand in everything. Illicit tobacco continues to fund crime syndicates, just what the Berettas are involved in."

Now it was Cheryl's turn to have a drink of water. Thomas watched as she took the drink without getting any of her red lipstick around the top of the bottle where her lips had been. He thought she must have on one of those budge-proof lipsticks that supermodels were always advertising on TV. "Well that's quite interesting, Thomas. Thank you, well done. Please do put it in a report for me."

Thomas smiled to himself, feeling proud. He wasn't about to tell Cheryl that Bianca had just pretty much blurted it all out to him. "I'm sorry I hadn't collated all the information before I came in. I'll get onto it ASAP and send it through." But the report wouldn't just be sent to Cheryl this time.

"And Stacey Klein - I haven't heard anything from either you or Bianca about her?" Cheryl looked questioningly at Thomas.

"Well to be honest Cheryl, Bianca and I haven't even started that job yet. I've been concentrating on the other."

"My God!" Cheryl exclaimed, shaking her head. "What do you guys do all day? You know I'm not paying you two just to sit around, drink coffee and fuck each other."

Thomas smiled and laughed a little. Cheryl didn't like his apparent lack of concern for the task. "I'm being serious, Thomas. What you do with Bianca in your own time is your business now. However, you are not on an hourly rate any more like you were before. With this role in The Department you are now on a salary. You're supposed to be earning your money."

"Like how you do what you want with Bianca in your own time?" Thomas sat back into his chair and folded his arms in front of him, as if he was the boss.

Cheryl just smiled back at him. "Thomas, I know how much you would love to join me and Bianca, but you need to keep focus. You've done well with your information acquirement regarding the Berettas; however, you and Bianca are supposed to be doing the other job together. You need to do that so she doesn't become sus; plus we need a new subject, and another girl would be good. It's a fucking sausage fest around here!"

Yeah, I bet another girl would be good, Thomas thought to himself, once again thinking of Cheryl's fondness for the finer species.

Cheryl continued, "I want both you and Bianca in here next week with hopefully some good news to report." Cheryl took another drink from her water bottle just as David knocked on the door and let himself into the office.

"Ah Christo, mate, good to see you," said David, screwing his nose up like a rat.

Thomas noticed the nose deformity and knew what had caused it. "Yeah David, Cheryl has a new perfume - Chanel No.7."

"No. 5," Cheryl corrected.

"Roger."

"Oh, Chanel No. 5, I must remember that..." David said, giving Thomas a secret *'Thanks mate'* look.

For once in her life, Cheryl seemed oblivious to what was going on.

"Are we done here now?" asked Thomas in a somewhat insubordinate manner.

"Yes, Thomas, we are. I'll see you in a week."

Thomas got up from the office chair and picked up his coat from the back of it and his laptop bag from the ground. He walked out of his boss's office, relieved to be breathing in some unscented air.

"David, do take a seat. We have some things to discuss..."

"Michael, it's Dr David Wiley from Melbourne."

"Yes, I understand the protocol. However, I felt I needed to talk to you myself. It's about The Agency down here..."

He who plots to do evil will be called a schemer.

Prov. 24:8

• CHAPTER 41 •

Outer Eastern Suburbs, Melbourne, Victoria

BIANCA WAS BRUSHING HER long brunette hair when the intercom buzzed. It was Thomas and he was actually on time.

Amazing, she thought, letting him into the Fort Knox that was her high-end apartment building.

"Is that for me?" Bianca asked excitedly.

"Of course. I thought I'd better get you a little something after what you gave me the other night."

"Thomas, you didn't have to ... but I'm glad you did," Bianca laughed as she took the bottle of her favourite red wine in one hand and put the other on Thomas's back as she leant in for a kiss on the cheek.

"Wow, something smells great," Thomas commented honestly.

"Yeah, well, Margaret gave me a few recipes and I thought I might have a go at her lamb stew. I finally brought myself to face the department store to buy a slow cooker." Bianca unscrewed the lid from the bottle of wine. She loved how most reds didn't have corks now. *Fuck that shit*, is what crossed her mind at the thought of having to waste time with a cork screw, just to have the damn thing probably break on you.

Thomas shook his head in disbelief. "Wow, Bianca, you really are different, aren't you? I mean you have no trouble putting on some big act in front of a whole heap of people, but you can't handle a shopping centre? Weird."

"Hey, we all have our shit. It just comes out in different ways, shapes and forms. And I did handle it. Managed to get myself the slow cooker, didn't I? They had a sale on too, so there was like a million people there. I wouldn't have gone there if I'd known there was a sale." Bianca took a big gulp of her wine. Thomas thought she must be thinking about her department store experience.

"Well, I'm glad you did, because as I said it does smell really good. You're a good cook."

"Thank you. But truthfully, I'm pretty shit for an Italian. I'm trying, though..."

"I think your *Nonna* would be proud," Thomas said, proud of himself for once again using an Italian word.

"My whole family is proud," Bianca rebutted, thinking she hadn't even spoken to her mother that year.

"Naturally," Thomas replied as he took a seat in his usual spot on the couch. Samson was nowhere to be seen. Bianca noticed

Thomas's sweeping gaze around the living room and into the kitchen.

"He's on my bed asleep."

Thomas didn't reply but instead asked her a question, calling out to the kitchen where she was checking the stew. "Hey baby, you know how you told me about the guys that raped you, well did your family take care of them? Did they?"

Bianca walked into the living room holding her glass of wine. She was wearing a short skirt and an oversized woollen sweater that was so large it looked like it was almost all she had on. Thomas liked it.

"Two of them have been taken care of, yes. The others, well they will be taken care of. It's all about timing, you know?"

Thomas nodded in agreement. "Yes, it's always definitely all about timing."

"You want to know something, Thomas?" Bianca asked him, still standing in the middle of the living room. Before Thomas even had a chance to answer, she continued, "Those guys that 'raped' me. Well, they didn't really rape me. I let them have really rough sex with me. I let it get completely out of control." Bianca almost had a smile on her face.

Once again, Bianca was lucky not to have red wine spat out all over her light-coloured couch. Thomas managed to swallow his mouthful before commenting. "What! You set them up? Why would you do that? A couple of them are dead now!"

Bianca walked over to the couch and sat down next to Thomas, placing her wineglass on the coffee table. "They deserved it.

You see, they thought it was okay to fuck everything on base in a skirt. Fuck, fuck away they did, and then called the girl a slut. What was good for one was not good for the other. Ultimate injustice and discrimination. Something had to be done about it."

"So you decided to do something about it?" Thomas asked, looking into Bianca's eyes.

"Yep. I made a decision to bring the motherfuckers down over my career. I'm a fucking Suffragette of the new order, if you ask me." Bianca took a big sip of her red wine, looking almost defiant.

"So let me get this right. Just because some guys were calling girls 'sluts', you decided you would report them to the Defence Force for rape, then let your family slowly kill them off one by one?"

"Thomas, you make it sound like they were innocent. They were not innocent. You don't call a girl a slut for just doing the same as her male counterpart is doing."

"I called you a slut, Bianca. During our rough sex, remember?"

"Yes, and I shot you, remember?" Bianca took another sip of her wine.

Wow, thought Thomas, the woman was actually dead serious.

Bianca put down her wineglass, moved her hand up under Thomas's shirt and rubbed his chest lightly. "It still hurts a little, doesn't it?" she asked in a slightly loving, yet masochistic manner.

"Yes, baby," Thomas replied as Bianca's hand moved down towards his groin, "It still does. A question though - does your family know that you made up the story about them raping you? I mean, that you actually set them up?"

"No, not at all. They think it happened. I needed them to, so they'd top them. The ADF did jack shit. All the men got was a slap over the wrist. Typical. But I can't dwell on that; at least I've got my uncles and brother to sort them out."

"What about your father?" Thomas asked. He was shocked, but at the same time intrigued at the conversation that had unfolded.

"My father is dead."

"I'm sorry to hear that," Thomas said, thinking how lucky he was to still have both parents alive and seemingly healthy.

"Thomas. It's fine. People live and then they die. Some earlier than others."

"And some not as early as you think?" Thomas said, looking Bianca directly in the eye despite her hand sitting over his nether regions.

"Obviously it wasn't your time, Thomas. What did I just say earlier? It's all about timing."

Thomas smiled at her and Bianca smiled back while rubbing him. "I'm glad it wasn't your time."

"Hey, what are those sticks over there?" Thomas asked, suddenly getting off the couch to have a closer inspection at the crafted pieces of rattan that had caught his attention.

Bianca was surprised at his sudden movement, especially given where her hand was on his pants. However, she answered, "Oh, they're Filipino Martial Arts sticks, a pair of *bastons*. Used for Arnis-Kali stick fighting."

Thomas walked over to the corner of the living room where the sticks were propped up, kind of on intentional display, and realised he hadn't noticed them before. He wondered if this was the first time Bianca had left them out on display or if they had always been sitting there. He picked up a stick, looking at the decorative engravings. He then tapped the stick against the palm of his hand.

"Ouch!" he cried, rubbing the palm of his hand. "That hurt!"

Bianca laughed. "Yeah, those *bastons* hurt like hell. They're designed not just to break bone, but to shatter it. Nasty little shits, those Filipinos."

CHAPTER 42

Outer Eastern Suburbs, Melbourne, Victoria

"YEAH, NASTY ALL RIGHT," Thomas replied, still rubbing his hand. "Why do you have these?"

"I've been training in Filipino martial arts for a number of years. Arnis, Kali, Eskrima, whatever you want to call it. Both weapons and open hands. I used to date a Filipino guy and he got me involved. Good for my anger management."

Thomas laughed. "Yeah, well we all need some of that." He walked back over to the coffee table, picked up his wine and took a sip, then said, "So you're pretty good then, hey?"

"I'm okay."

"Okay for a girl," Thomas teased.

"No, I'm just okay," Bianca retorted, starting to be a little pissed at Thomas's tone.

"Well, why don't you show me how okay you are, then?" Thomas mocked.

"Is that a challenge, Mr Christian? Because if it is, then you are on." Bianca looked him straight in the eye.

Thomas smiled to himself. He loved when she called him Mr Christian. It meant she was becoming annoyed at him in the best possible way.

"Oh Bianca, challenge accepted. You are going down ... and not in the way you want to." Thomas couldn't help but say that.

Bianca laughed once again, throwing her head back. This time she looked more like The Evil Queen than Snow White. She got off the couch, headed to the corner and picked up the fighting sticks. She threw one *baston* to Thomas, who caught it in his hand.

"Hold on," Bianca said, "Let me put the wineglasses in the kitchen."

She's always thinking, thinking. Thinking too much, Thomas thought to himself.

Bianca returned to the living room holding the stick. Thomas moved in and took a swipe at her with his own stick, but Bianca manoeuvred her body right in towards him, quickly blocking the strike by striking her own left forearm against his right and snaking her arm around his forearm and wrist. Then in one swift movement she pulled back, forcing the stick out of Thomas's grasp, disarming him.

"Ha ha," Bianca said in a childlike tone. "And now I have two sticks and you have none."

"Well, it is a bit unfair." Thomas retaliated. "You've been trained with those sticks. I never have. Of course I know how to use a baton, but that is completely different. Unarmed, however, it will be a different story for you. I'll restrain you in three seconds."

Bianca dropped the sticks. "We'll see."

Thomas smiled, thinking the fun was about to begin. Bianca was at least thirty kilos lighter than him.

She moved in quicker than Thomas was expecting and she was right in at his body, giving him no distance. In an instant she had executed an open palm upper cut under his chin followed by an elbow across his face. Bianca's heel had gone into his shin and she had slid it all the way down his shin and into his foot.

Thomas took a couple of steps back with one hand on his eyebrow, that was bleeding where Bianca had opened it up with her sharp elbow.

"Bianca, what the fuck? We were only supposed to grapple! You weren't supposed to strike me, for fuck's sake."

"Oh baby, I'm sorry," Bianca said, sounding as if she was holding in laughter. "I didn't know. Lack of communication. We're both to blame. Maybe we should have talked about some rules before we decided to play?"

"You think?" Thomas said, still covering the eyebrow cut and with the other hand rubbing his bruised shin.

"Here, let me go get some antiseptic cream for that cut. It'll help stop it bleeding and heal it up."

Bianca returned with a tube of Hirudoid cream. It reminded Thomas of the times when he had come off his bike as a child. The Hirudoid cream always seemed to make an appearance.

"I'm sorry baby, I really didn't mean to hurt you," Bianca said, rubbing some cream onto Thomas's dark eyebrow.

"It's okay, because now I'm going to get you back," and with that Thomas grabbed Bianca's arm and wrapped it up behind her back so he had control of her. He pushed her up against the kitchen bench and bent her slightly over it while taking control of her other arm. He knew better than to trust her with one arm still free to do as it pleased. Years of training and real-life experience had come instantly into play and he could tell he had a good lock on her. He could actually see the frustration on her face as she realised she was helpless.

"Less than three seconds, I reckon," Thomas laughed.

Bianca sighed and stopped any struggle. She was in just the position she wanted to be in.

"Ha, you giving up that easy, are you?" Thomas teased.

Looking straight ahead at her slow cooker, thinking maybe it was time for the thing to be turned off, Bianca replied: "No point fighting against you, Thomas. I mean, even my bullet couldn't take you down. I might as well give up."

"That's a girl," Thomas replied. He pulled up her skirt and then pulled down her black lace panties. "You are just going to have to take what is served out to you."

I always do, Bianca thought to herself, *and I always get myself into the best positions for it.*

"You hungry?" Bianca asked Thomas, who was now sitting up at the kitchen bench with a fresh glass of red wine.

"Well, after that exertion of energy, I'm ravenous."

Bianca smiled and started serving the stew onto a plate for the man.

Thomas could feel his work phone vibrating. He pulled it out of his pocket and looked at the screen. It was from a phone number he didn't recognise. He thought he'd best answer it.

"I'm sorry, Bianca. Be back in a tick, I just need to answer this…" and with that Thomas walked out of her apartment and down the hall.

"Yes, this is Thomas Christian, who is asking? … Oh yes sir, I'm sorry… Certainly, I have a moment… I understand, sir. I will, sir. Yes, now I have your number. Yes, if any questions… Okay then. Will do."

Thomas knocked on Bianca's door and she let him back in. He was again struck by how great the stew smelled.

"You were gone for ages. I thought you might have done the runner on me," Bianca said in a tone that sounded a little bit too much like his wife's.

Thomas smiled at his lover. "No way, that stew smells way too good for that."

"Little shit," Bianca replied, striking him lightly with the tea towel she was holding.

"Hey, you know you love it," Thomas replied. "Plus, don't even start that again with me," referring to the tea towel strike. "You know what just happened, don't you?"

Bianca once again flicked the tea towel against him, but this time harder at the back of his legs.

"Oh, you really do love it don't you, Bianca?"

The woman just smiled and thought, *Yes, yes I do.*

CHAPTER 43

Inner City, Melbourne, Victoria

B IANCA COULDN'T HELP BUT think how good Thomas looked standing at the bar of the happening nightclub. He may have been twenty years older than the majority of men in the joint, but in her opinion he was by far the one she would most want to take home. She thought herself lucky for having him as her work colleague and lover, despite how twisted the relationship was.

"Thank you," she said, as Thomas handed her a wine.

"No worries. Probably won't be very nice. I think it's just cheap house wine."

"Well, it has to be better than what you're drinking," Bianca said, looking at Thomas's bourbon filled with post-mix cola. "Yuk. Cola's bad enough at the best of times, but post-mix, that is just gross."

Thomas took a sip of his drink. "Yeah, it sucks." He squirmed up his face in disgust. "I think my next will be on the rocks."

He took a seat next to Bianca who was propped up on the high nightclub stool. She was wearing her highest leather boots - or in Thomas's language, her "Come Fuck Me Boots." She looked hot and Thomas saw that she knew it too.

The pair sat quietly sipping their drinks and covertly scanning the club for Stacey Klein.

"Why do they have to play the music so loud?" Thomas said, sounding like his own father.

"The young ones don't think it's loud," replied Bianca. "At least there's no smoking any more. Remember how everyone used to smoke in the nightclubs and you'd wake up in the morning stinking of cigarette smoke? It used to stick to my hair and I'd have to wash my hair, otherwise I'd smell like an astray for the following week."

Thomas nodded his head in agreement. "Yeah, well at least that's something the government did get right." He took another sip of his bourbon, finishing it off. He was glad to see the bottom of the glass. He then continued, "They should make smoking illegal altogether."

Bianca smiled and Thomas computed what he had actually said. "I would love for them to ban tobacco smoking altogether, my family would be *very* happy. You know, supply and demand."

Thomas stared into Bianca's eyes and he swore he could see the dollar signs in them. She apparently wasn't involved with the business herself, but she obviously still reaped some of the rewards.

Suddenly the song *Give It Back* filled the nightclub, vibrations bouncing off the walls. "I freaking love this song, let's go dance!" Bianca grabbed Thomas's hand to try to pull him up off his stool and onto the dance floor. The man didn't budge.

"Dance? No way. I don't dance. Plus we're supposed to be working."

"Ha, typical. Well, I'm going out there." And with that Bianca walked onto the dance floor and started to dance in 'I know I'm hot' female style. It didn't seem to bother her that she was essentially dancing by herself amongst the crowd of the dance floor. Thomas quickly realised that she needn't be bothered because within the minute, she had a few guys trying to dance with her. The guys looked about fifteen years Bianca's junior and Thomas thought they were probably Army, given their military-looking haircuts, large faced G- Shock watches and lack of individual style.

Thomas watched on, not taking his eyes off Bianca. Stacey Klein could have entered the club and he wouldn't have seen her. He watched how Bianca danced as if the guys weren't there, acting nonchalant and entranced in herself and the music. But he knew for a fact that Bianca was very much aware of the men and their intentions.

The song had ended and another came on. Bianca kept dancing. One of the braver men moved in closer to her and lightly put one of his hands on her waist. Bianca leaned in and said something to him. The man laughed and continued to try to dance with her.

All of a sudden, Thomas was standing next to Bianca. "Don't even try it, mate," Thomas said to the braver of the guys.

"Fuck off," was the young soldier's reply.

"Trust me. This one is mine. If you don't leave her alone, I'll break off your legs at the knees, put them in your ears and ride you around like a bicycle. Understood?" Thomas looked dead serious. Bianca had to hold the laughter in.

"Fuck, all right then." The guy walked off and joined his mates, who had moved a few metres away. "Slut," he muttered as he walked away.

Both Bianca and Thomas heard it. Bianca looked furious and Thomas knew he had to take control before the guy got a glassing from her.

He grabbed her and said, "Leave it. He's just a boy, he has no idea."

"He's fucking lucky..." Bianca replied with crazy woman eyes. "Only because we're on the job. If we weren't I'd have given him a new face."

"See? This is what happens when you go off and dance like that - you attract the wolves," Thomas said, referring to the pack.

"No Thomas, they're sheep in wolves' clothing. I am the wolf," and with that Bianca headed straight to the bar to get herself another wine.

After a few minutes, Bianca returned to their vantage point within the night spot. "On the rocks, just for you," Bianca said as she handed over the drink she'd brought back for him. Thomas admired how quickly she had seemed to get over the dancefloor almost–altercation. Then he remembered that although she seemed to get over things, she never forgot them. She locked them into her vault to be dealt with later. The boy was very fortunate he had only had a passing-by with Bianca.

"Thanks. Hey, what did you say to that bloke to make him laugh when you were dancing?"

"I told him I was way above his pay rate," answered Bianca.

"There she is," Thomas suddenly said, apparently not registering Bianca's answer.

"Where?" Bianca asked, pissed off that Thomas had spotted Stacey Klein before her.

"Ten o'clock in the white dress."

Bianca looked at the attractive girl with long blonde hair. She sure was a petite thing, short and small framed. Bianca thought how much Cheryl would like her. *She obviously has no common sense, though*, thought Bianca, because of the white dress the woman was wearing in a night club where the majority of punters were drinking red or brown drinks.

"She's cute. Even better than her photo, I think. What do you think? You think she's cute?" Thomas asked, eager for Bianca's answer.

"Yeah, she's cute."

Thomas looked happy with the reply. Bianca continued, "But we're not going to recommend her as a subject. We already agreed on that. The girl's been through enough; she doesn't need to be used by The Department as part of their sicko experiment."

"Absolutely agreed, but that doesn't mean we still can't have some fun with her ourselves, does it?" Thomas asked with blue puppy-dog eyes.

Bianca knew how much Thomas wanted to have a three-way with her, and she knew how important it was to keep the man interested. His wife and Bianca together were completely out of the question, and Cheryl didn't show any signs of interest in it, either. By the look of Stacey and her lack of common sense, she would be willing.

Bianca leaned in and gave Thomas a kiss, then whispered in his ear, "Let me do the talking." With that she made her way over to Stacey Klein, who was standing at the bar with another friend. Before Thomas knew it, Stacey was walking over to Thomas holding Bianca's hand.

Fuck me, that woman is good, he thought through his excitement at the unfolding situation.

"Thomas, this is Stacey. I told Stacey about you and she wanted to meet you."

"Hi," Stacey said shyly, looking away.

"He's good looking, isn't he? Why don't you sit up on his lap?" Bianca urged the young woman.

Stacey let go of her hand and propped herself up on Thomas. Thomas looked exactly how he felt – like one very lucky man. Bianca couldn't help but see the flash of Stacey's white knickers as she sat down on Thomas's lap up on the high stool. The thought of having some young sweetness sent tingles down Bianca's body and for a moment she pondered on a thought: *who were the real sickos, The Department... or her and Thomas?*

CHAPTER 44

Carlton, Melbourne, Victoria

D AVID HADN'T BEEN SLEEPING well lately and last night had been no exception. Despite the near freezing temperatures of his cold Victorian terrace, he had woken in a sweat. The house had heating, but David was such a tight arse he used it as little as possible.

His decision to go above Cheryl and speak with Michael had been playing on his mind. He was questioning his own decision making. He had never felt bad about his involvement with The Department's Agency project. He had actually thought it was a pretty good idea, as something had to be done with these types of people; plus it paid okay. However, he had thought he would have progressed within The Department by now. Cheryl's complete lack of recommendation for any pay increase or promotion for him, along with the fact that she was a control freak who seemed to be getting completely out of control and was compromising his own position, had all contributed to his decision.

David was still a little in shock about what Michael had told him. He thought he knew Cheryl, but apparently, he didn't know her at all. Everything, had all been one big act. *She really did miss her calling. She would have been a star of both screen and stage,* he couldn't help but think. He deliberated on how she could have used her skills to entertain people, rather than on working her own agenda. It was however, too late for that now. Her past had finally caught up with her.

As much as he liked Thomas, he was still unsure of the man and his capabilities. As had been reported in the past, he was a 'complete live wire' and he could never really be trusted. With Thomas, what you saw was not necessarily what you got. David thought that Christo knew how to play the game even more than Bianca. Life was a game to him - and he was an expert player. David just hoped that he could be trusted with this one. If this job didn't go down to plan, then fuck knows what would happen to himself. He shuddered at the thought as he poured milk onto his Coco Pops. He swirled around the milk and cereal until he had created the cereal's slogan line. He looked around his small unrenovated kitchen and noticed that a crack in the corner near the ceiling seemed to have become bigger overnight. He wondered how long he could leave it before having to get in a plasterer to undertake repairs.

Hmm, maybe I could try to fix it myself? he thought as he piled a heap of the breakfast milkshake onto his spoon and into his mouth.

Outer Eastern Suburbs, Melbourne, Victoria

"*Ciao*, Margaret," Bianca said down the line of her phone.

"Ah, Bianca. How are you?"

"I'm okay, Margaret. How are you?"

"Good, good. I'm just in the middle of making some gnocchi."

"Oh yum. I would love some gnocchi," stated Bianca thinking of her insatiable appetite at the moment.

"Yes, well you should give it a go. I gave you the recipe, you know."

"Yeah, well I haven't tried that one, but I have been trying a few. It's just time. They take so much time, all the prep and everything, and so many ingredients," said Bianca, thinking how more ingredients equalled more time at the local supermarket, her least favourite place in the world.

"You just need to build up your pantry, so you have most of the ingredients stocked. I can't just duck down to the local store from out here; I have to have things ready at hand."

"Yeah, I know, I should be more onto it. How's *Zio*?"

"He's doing well, he's not at the house at the moment, though. He's with the *horses*..."

"Oh, I see. How are the *horses* doing?" Bianca asked, with interest.

"Well, so far this year, the *horses* are coming along well."

"So plenty of *foals* then, for the season?"

"Yes, well as you know, the season never stops." Both women laughed down the line.

"I'm sorry to ask, but have you spoken with your mother lately?" Margaret asked a little hesitantly.

Bianca coughed then replied, "You're not sorry at all. No, I haven't spoken with her lately. She has my number is she wants to call. If she wants to apologise..."

The line was silent for a moment before Margaret responded, "I don't know if that will happen, Bianca. You may need to be the bigger person. She's not a Beretta. You are though; you may need to be the initiator of the conversation."

"She can't handle the conversation. She can't handle anything without him. Fucking babbling mess." Bianca paused, then continued apologetically, "Sorry Margaret, I didn't mean to swear in front of you."

"That's okay. I know you didn't mean to. I understand that she upsets you."

"Well, yeah. After being blamed for Dad's death, that I brought the heart attack on; well yes, she did upset me. Who does that? Who treats their daughter like that?"

"Jealousy, Bianca," Margaret replied with confidence.

"Excuse me?" Bianca asked surprised.

"She was jealous. She is jealous. It's actually not uncommon, you know, mother-daughter rivalry."

Bianca deliberated on Margaret's words before answering. Finally she said, "Well that is just twisted. What type of person is that twisted?"

"The person who made you, Bianca."

Margaret realised what she had said and hoped that Bianca didn't take offence. To Margaret's delight, Bianca seemed to ignore the comment and changed the subject.

"So how's my girl Caterina?" Bianca asked of the horse she had been given by her aunt and uncle, that was now agisted at the farm.

"Your filly is good. She's looking in fine form. We are giving her lots of attention." Bianca thought she could almost hear Margaret smiling down the phone line.

"Yes, well that's good. They need a lot of attention, all horses."

"You going to come ride her soon? I think she would like that," the aunt both asked and stated to her niece.

"I would like that too, but I don't know if I should. Actually, that's why I rang..."

CHAPTER 45

South Melbourne, Victoria

B IANCA AND THOMAS HAD both arrived at their place of work at the same time. Bianca was impressed that Thomas was on time for the meeting. Cheryl had wanted a thorough situation report from them regarding their studies of the potential subject, Stacey Klein.

The administration girl looked up as Thomas and Bianca entered the main office area of The Agency. They walked past her desk. "Morning, Bianca. Morning, Thomas" she said in an overly cheerful voice. Bianca ignored her. Thomas replied, "Morning, Katie." Katie smiled, obviously happy at the acknowledgment.

"So I got all the report typed out," Bianca informed Thomas as they walked towards Cheryl's office. She had taken responsibility for the report. She knew her report writing was of a higher standard than Thomas's. *No wonder he's struggling to write a novel,* she thought to herself. Bianca continued the conversation: "It's just as we discussed. You know, based on our studies we believe Stacey would not be a good candidate for the Agency project for a multitude of reasons. The main one being her age, the others being her lack of common sense, her lack of problem solving abilities, her inability to falsify facts and think on the spot; oh yeah, and her shyness."

"Well, she wasn't exactly shy with us, was she?" Thomas remarked, thinking about the girl's lips on him while he had his lips on another part of Bianca.

Bianca laughed. "Well, no, she wasn't. We were just what she needed, I think. Obviously, I did falsify some things."

"You always do, don't you?" asked Thomas as they entered Cheryl's office.

Bianca didn't get a chance to answer him as Cheryl spoke as soon as they had walked through the door. "Well, you two. I'm anticipating a good news report." The smell in the room was the same as the week before. Thomas thought he would be glad to never have to smell that perfume again.

David was standing in the office near the doorway that he had suddenly closed. Bianca noticed he looked more agitated than usual.

Thomas turned and looked at Bianca, ignoring Cheryl's comment. "Bianca, how do you kill a snake?"

Given the context of the situation, Bianca thought it an unusual question however she answered. She knew the answer as she had seen many a snake killed, growing up in country Victoria. "You cut off its head."

"Yes," replied Thomas. "Remember that."

Without any other warning, Thomas pulled out a knife blade

that had been concealed in a sheath positioned in the small of his back and covered by his jacket. Before she had a chance to get up from her seat, Thomas moved behind Cheryl's chair and slid the blade across her throat in one swift clean movement. Blood immediately started to run from the boss's throat.

Bianca looked on stunned. She had seen a throat cut before and that vision came flashing back to her. Thomas had executed Cheryl just the way she had seen her family undertake executions. Clearly stunned by this unexpected turn of events, Bianca said: "This wasn't part of the plan, Thomas. You won't get away with this. The Department will come after you. You're a dead man."

"Bianca, who do you think asked me to do this? When Canberra asked, I could only say yes. You're not the only one that can be compliant. The bitch deserved it, she was out to destroy The Department."

"The Department? The Department asked you to?" Bianca spluttered.

"Yes, they did. And there's something else I have to do," said Thomas, grabbing Bianca in one of his specialised restraints and forcing her right hand on the office table near Cheryl's now lifeless body.

"Thomas baby, you said you would never lay a finger on me, not a finger," Bianca cried with tears welling up in her eyes.

"I lied," and with that Thomas held down the hand tightly and sliced off her right trigger finger below the joint. Bianca screamed and grabbed her hand, bringing it in close to her chest to try to contain the bleeding as the blood started covering her designer sweater. Her knees fell weak, and Bianca suddenly found herself seated on the floor of the office.

"You see, Bianca, you thought you knew me, but you really didn't know me at all..."

Bianca looked at him with absolute sadness and horror. Her eyes were swollen red and for a moment Thomas thought she looked like a little girl. Bianca then spoke, not sounding sad, but ferocious. "You are truly stupid, aren't you? You won't get away with it. My family, they'll hunt you down. You'll be the one ending up in pieces in some bin."

Thomas smiled and chuckled lightly. "That's where you're wrong, Bianca. You see, everyone including you seemed to forget who I used to work for. It pays to keep those contacts," stated Thomas with a smile, thinking of the phone call he had received earlier that morning about the raid at the farm.

"Mother fucker," Bianca managed to spit back at Thomas. She was now once again in tears and holding her right hand tightly. "And what am I supposed to do now?"

"Well that's your problem, not mine. You create your own destiny, Bianca. You said it was all about timing. I say it's all about choices," and with that Thomas walked out of the room, leaving Bianca seated on the floor with a mixture of her own and Cheryl's blood pooling around her.

Bianca looked up at David for some help. Her eyes were the size of saucers. He was still standing near the doorway of Cheryl's office. His face was white and he looked as if he might faint at any moment. He did, however, manage to maintain his composure.

"I'm in charge now, Bianca. My boss, Michael Croaker, has promoted me. That was Thomas's last assignment within The Department. We asked him to do it and we needed him to do it. She had leaked information, Bianca. Information from her previous department and from this project. I'm sorry about your finger; I actually didn't know he was going to do that to you. I guess he didn't want to be shot again..."

"What about my family? Did The Department authorise that too?" Bianca looked fierce, but David knew she was in no state to take any action.

"Bianca, there's no need to worry about your family. Even though Cheryl didn't know, The Department knew all about your family. You of all people should have known that your family is in cahoots with the law. You understand the depths of police corruption at the highest level. What Thomas thinks happened and what actually happened are two different things. Your family can continue business as usual and you can continue your work here."

"I'm not working for fucking you, or the fucking Department or the fucking Government ever again! You're all a bunch of cunts!" Bianca cried as blood continued to run down her hand and onto her chest, covering her sweater even more.

"I understand that you may feel that way right now. However, you have two choices. Leave now and you'll be the victim. Sure, you could get your family to do your dirty work, but don't you want to do it *yourself*? If you stay The Department will protect you. I'll protect you..." Bianca thought David sounded like a desperate child sex offender trying to rope in his next victim. Unfortunately, she knew which option needed to be taken for the moment. He continued, "Once your finger heals, I might even put you onto a special job, one in which you may be able to pay it forward..."

Bianca managed a slight smile, still trying to stop the heavy bleeding from her finger. She also noticed she was bleeding through the crotch of her jeans, "He'll get more than paid forward..." Bianca managed to say before passing out.

Inner Eastern Suburbs, Melbourne, Victoria

"Hi Jody, I'm home."

"Hi honey, I'm so glad you're home."

"So am I," said Thomas, lifting his wife off the ground and spinning her around a little.

"Wow, you are glad. Why so happy?" she asked with a large smile.

"I quit my job today."

The smile left her face and Jody looked immediately concerned. She didn't want to have to give up Alda's private schooling or her own tennis lessons.

Thomas read the look on his wife's face. "Don't worry. We have plenty of money until I find something else. I've been putting some away for a rainy day." He thought of the big cheque that was promised to him by The Department upon completion of his final job.

"Oh honey, that's good to hear. I know that family comes first to you. What are you going to do in the meantime while you're looking for something else?"

"Finish my book."

"You got something to write about now?" Jody asked, sounding interested for the first time since Thomas had started the manuscript.

"I certainly do," Thomas replied with a knowing smile.